We Will Never Leave You, Baby Girl

An MDLG and DDLG story about Alice, an ABDL little who completed her Mommy and Daddy's lives

Tina Moore

Table of Contents

Chapter 1

"When are you going to grow up?" His words struck her like a punch to the gut, followed closely by a wave of white-hot anger. He had known exactly where to target his words - precisely known how to bait her. Alice had walked right into it. She had shown her vulnerability to him. She had opened up, and that had proven to be a massive error in judgment time and time again.

Alice ran her hands through her dark hair, scraping her scalp with her fingernails. She gripped fistfuls of it and held it there, tightening her grip as she fought to restrain herself from physically assaulting him. She sighed and dropped her hands again. Alice had tried to explain it to him a few times before, but he didn't seem quite to understand. Or he didn't want to understand. She could feel tears well up and sting her eyes. No way was she going to allow him to make her cry again, not this time. She had given him so many chances, but David couldn't see past her freakish childish behavior (his words, not hers). She wasn't a freak. She just liked being taken care of. She needed to be taken care of.

"You're a grown-ass adult. It's time to act like it. I'm not here to take care of some bratty bitch," his words cut through her thoughts, setting her resolve.

"Nice," Alice said dryly.

"What? It's fucking true," David shouted. They stared at each other for half a second in tense, angry silence before she took a deep breath.

"Fine," Alice plainly said.

"What?" David questioned, annoyed, and wanting to hurt her.

"I'm done," Alice clenched her jaw and shut down her emotions. That was her go-to. She would deal with the fallout later. Right now, she was fighting it so she could get herself out of there.

"What are you talking about?" David

aggressively questioned.

"I'm leaving, David," Alice softly replied.

"You can't just leave in the middle of a fight, Alice!" The furry in his eyes made Alice's stomach churn.

"Watch me," Alice said, snatching her keys off of the coffee table and stomping to the door as he threw every name in the book at her. She let his words wash over her but kept her composure as best she could.

"You'll never be happy, Alice, because no one will want you. Ever," David had driven the final blade as deep as he could. Alice knew it was because his ego had been hurt, but she couldn't let this one slide. She wheeled to face him, the door open with her hand grasping the knob, "Excuse me?"

"You're broken. You can't function alone, and you know it," David remarked, impressed with the pain he was causing her. The color drained from her face. David's smirk twisted the knife in her gut, "You're stuck in your messed-up past." Alice could feel her anger flash through her. It threatened to form her hand into a fist at the end of her arm as she slammed the door behind her. She took the stairs down as fast as she could, placing as much distance between them before she did something stupid like punching him in his obnoxious face.

She sat in the driver's seat of her car. She was shaking, holding on to her tenuous emotions that were roiling around inside of her like white rapids. She knew David was less than accommodating to her lifestyle, as he had put it, but Alice had thought that he would be able to get over it. She had thought that he would eventually just get used to Alice retreating into her little space on occasion. He had even seemed into it the first few times. When aftercare was required, he had mysteriously remembered that he had some errand to run. Eventually, he had stopped coming up with excuses and simply refused. She should have gotten out then, but of course, Alice had stubbornly held out with a vague hope that he would change.

David had known which buttons to push to make her hurt because she had given him the ammunition and painted a giant target on her back. They had been together for a year - one long, unsatisfying, stressful year, and she had let him in.

It amazed her that she had stayed with him for so long. At that moment, Alice knew that she had never intended to be with him for the amount of time that she had. She had only stayed with him out of—what? Desperation? Loneliness? Alice clenched her teeth, jammed the key in the ignition, and tore out of the parking lot. If only she could run away from her thoughts and feelings as quickly as she could escape David. Alice hated that she couldn't stand to be alone. She hated that David could even remotely be right.

By the time Alice pulled her small, dinged-up car into the parking lot of her less-than-ideal apartment block, tears had already drawn black streaks down her cheeks. Smudges made worse by her wiping at the tears as they fell. It was late in the afternoon on a Friday. Alice sat in her car, watching the neighborhood kids running around, laughing, utterly oblivious to the world around them. Alice wanted to be just as carefree, just as—just as happy, she decided. But whenever she exposed her little side, she had the wind knocked out of her. First Vi, then Danielle, and now David. Alice couldn't' blame them. She hadn't been exactly open with them about her needs.

She closed her eyes and took a deep, steadying breath. Her tears were still running down her face. There was no stopping the dam from breaking anymore, and it was only a matter of time before she knew her phone would ping non-stop. She knew without looking that it would be David. Every fight that had ended in Alice leaving his place resulted in his angry, pleading, and often crazy messages.

Alice wiped at another stray tear and finally made her way to her apartment, kicking the car door shut with her boot and shrugging her purse over her shoulder.

It was small, but it was home, and it was hers. Alice had painstakingly cleaned every scuff mark, scrubbed the carpet within an inch of fraying the fibers. It was clean, tidy, and it always smelled sweet and fruity.

Her phone pinged again as she dumped her stuff on the kitchen counter.

"Oh my God," Alice growled, gritting her teeth, "Will you leave me alone?" She opened the messages, reading through each one.

Babe, I'm sorry

Let's talk

You're a bitch

I don't know why I said that. I'll try to get better at this

Give me another chance

Ping. The screen scrolled up as each new message filled the page with black lines.

You'll come back, I know it. You just can't stay away

Ping.

Fuck you, Alice

Ping. Frustrated and angry, Alice threw herself

and her phone onto her bed facedown, stifling a groan with the bundle of messy bedsheets balled in her fists. Her moan slowly turned into another sob that got stuck in her throat. She turned her head sideways and allowed her mouth room to breathe.

It would be easy to go back. It would be so simple just to pick up where they left off. She had done it before.

"Fuck him," Alice said to herself.

She pushed herself up, grabbed everything that was scattered around, and shoved all of it into the washing hamper. After a minute, she realized that some of David's clothes had ended up in there as well. She hastily pulled those pieces out, sending shirts and boxers flying everywhere. She swore again, angrily picking up pieces of clothing and trying to avoid letting David's stuff touch hers.

Alice sat down on the floor in defeat, burying her hands in her hair with her head on her knees. She had invited David over a couple of times throughout their relationship, but he rarely stayed the night.

"I don't like the kid stuff," he had commented off-handedly, pulling his boots back on after she had given him what he wanted. The feelings of abandonment had welled up in her again, as David waltzed out of her apartment.

She had gone to his place the next morning seeking comfort, and they had fallen in bed together again. It never went further than that. Bringing it up only made him angry, and their relationship was new, so she felt vulnerable.

He didn't care for the aftercare portion of their activities, and eventually, Alice had stopped pushing. Enough time had passed that she'd kept that part of herself hidden as far away from him as possible, only rarely breaking. Yet still, she had gotten rapped over the knuckles.

Alice allowed the tears to flow, and the sobbing sounds to tear from her throat. They came from deep within her, drawing upon the loneliness she felt. It wasn't like she missed him—not really. But she didn't like being alone, and now that David was out of her life, the reminder that she had no one had come crashing home, the force strong enough to break her.

The weight of her emotions threatened to crush her as Alice lay down, curling in on herself on the thinly carpeted floor. She stuffed fistfuls of duvet into her mouth to stifle her wails. The dam had been broken.

Eventually, the tears stopped falling, and her sobs drained out of her, transforming into light hiccoughs. She remained in her curled position, with her head against her knees for a while longer, feeling the hollowness left behind by the anger and sorrow. She tilted her head so she could glance around the room, darkness having invaded in the absence of light.

She inhaled shakily and pushed herself into a seated position again. Alice stared at the closet doors, unblinking as she struggled with her mind telling her to leave it be. Alice wanted to get rid of everything that made her different, but she shoved that thought away.

There wasn't space in her already overfilled, overstressed brain to feel weird about her kink.

She sighed, wiped at her eyes, and methodically started cleaning up her scattered life. Every so often, Alice would burst into tears again as she remembered David's words assaulted her. They had been what Alice was already thinking, and it rubbed her the wrong way that he could be right.

She pulled herself together and finally cleaned the rest of her small apartment, tossing David's things into a garbage bag and leaving it by the front door. Alice pulled the sheets off her bed and stuffed everything else into the hamper along with it.

When she was satisfied with the bareness of her room, she went to the small bathroom that was hidden by a closet door. The design had struck Alice as odd, but she had gotten used to it over the years. She assumed that owners of the apartment block had intended to save money by breaking into a small storage room through her closet instead of ripping the whole wall out to remodel the old building.

She sat on the edge of the bath, popped the plug into the hole, and turned on the water. Alice poured a very generous dollop of sweetpea-scented bubble bath into the running stream. She wiped at the moisture on her face and watched the bubbles grow and foam as the warm water filled the tub. She dropped a small bright orange bath bomb in the water and deeply inhaled the sweet citrus scent as it fizzed and bobbed, turning the water orange. She smiled as the glitter swirled through the bubbles. Alice turned the water off and stripped herself of her clothes, kicking them into a pile in the corner of the bathroom. She would deal with that later.

She brushed her hands through her dark hair and pouted at the puffy-eyed reflection of herself as the bathroom filled with steam and the scent of blossoms and soapy bubbles. She carefully removed her industrial and her septum piercings and set them into the cup sitting on the sink. Alice smiled at her reflection, then shook her head. She pulled a face, baring her teeth at herself. She giggled and poured a little cleaning solution into the cup. She dampened a clump of cotton wool and washed the tiny pinpricks where she had just removed the piercings.

Alice smiled again at her reflection, feeling her body relax slowly. She carefully washed her face, getting rid of the smeared streaks of mascara. Her dark, deep red lipstick followed the same fate. She admired herself for a moment, her big, green, cat-like eyes looking back at her. She might not have been classically beautiful, but she had that edgy beauty that captivated people.

Alice happily hummed as she half-danced, half-wiggled in place as she pulled her long hair up into a knot. The bright pink under-color was finally exposed. Alice grinned and stuffed her hair into a flowery shower cap. She walked naked to her portable speaker and plugged her phone into the jack. She hit shuffle and danced her way back to the bathroom as her favorite songs filled the apartment.

She tested the water, goosebumps spreading over her exposed skin. She slid into the warmth and delighted in the way the remaining bath bomb fizzed between her toes. Alice laughed as she slid unexpectedly a little deeper beneath the water in the slippery tub and sighed happily. Alice scooped a palm-full of bubbles and blew them into the air, watching the tiniest ones swirl and fall slowly back down. She allowed her body to sink even deeper beneath the water until the bubbles tickled her nose. Alice blew hard into the foam covering her lips and giggled at the small spray as the foam exploded outward.

She spent enough time in the bath to turn her fingers wrinkly and the water uncomfortably cold. Alice wrapped herself in a soft, fluffy towel, rubbing the fabric over her skin. She could feel some tears welling up again, but took a few deep, steadying breaths and forced those emotions away. She liked being who she was, and she wasn't going to let an ass like David bully her into changing.

She walked back to her room and dug through the box of things in the back of her closet and found her favorite blankie. Alice also pulled her stuffed giant koala out of the box.

"Beanie!" She exclaimed, delighted, snuggling him close to her breast. He was nearly half her size and incredibly soft. She'd gotten Beanie on a whim when she had first moved in. Alice felt a tug from deep inside of her, a comforting safety that allowed her to sink into the warmth of his curly fur completely. Alice closed her eyes and held him for a moment.

Inside was a bunch of her little clothes, ribbons, and coloring things. Alice tucked Beanie onto her lap as she rummaged through the box, carefully unpacking everything she had hidden from David. She pulled her paci out and went to rinse it off in the sink before putting it in her mouth. She had come across tubes of paint and laughed as she squeezed a blob onto her finger and smeared it across the edge of the box. She did the same thing with each of the colors and drew an abstract picture that vaguely looked like a fat, rainbow-colored penguin.

She felt her whole body unwinding, releasing the tension she had been holding in. Alice tried to wipe away as much of the paint as possible on the box, letting the rest dry as she hummed.

She stroked Beanie's fur and hummed to herself.

She lay down on her stomach, still hugging Beanie tightly beneath one arm. Alice had taken out one of her favorite coloring books and turned to a random page. On it was a beach scene with a couple of puppies, a giant beach ball, and a crumpled, sand-covered blanket. Alice poured the box of wax crayons out on the bedroom floor and carefully chose the perfect color for the beach blanket.

She was halfway through when she decided to color one of the dogs a bright pink and wrote Strawbs as small as possible in the space that was meant to be the collar.

Without realizing it, Alice had begun drifting off to sleep. The week had been long and hard, and the drama of the day had drained her of the rest of her energy.

Alice startled awake, the light still on, crayon in hand. She yawned, dropped the crayon, and crawled into her bed with Beanie held close.

***

Alice woke, her dark hair messy, and her eyes were struggling to open in the late morning light. She had stayed up long past her usual bedtime, making a mess of her room as she dug through the boxes of things she had hidden in the back of her closet.

She spent the rest of the morning and most of the afternoon in bed, scrolling through YouTube and Instagram, looking at how her favorite creators repainted old dolls and made them new clothes. Alice loved watching them get their tiny makeovers, from their fresh faces to the brand new hairstyles and their teeny-tiny outfits. The dolls were pre-loved, their hair knotted and dirty, and their plastic faces smeared with muck and some form of colored marker.

It reminded her that no matter how messed up something might be. It could still be made beautiful.

Alice snuggled Beanie and pressed play on the next video. She didn't want to get up yet, even though she knew she had to send out her resume if she wanted to find something that paid better.

Alice had fallen asleep again, waking up when the sun had already dipped below the horizon. Her stomach growled unhappily, and she rolled out of bed, logging into a delivery app for dinner. She spent the rest of the night eating Chinese takeout and scrolling through Instagram.

Early on Sunday morning, Alice woke feeling less fragile and took a quick shower.

She organized her room and threw the empty box in the trash. She wouldn't have to hide her little things anymore. She smiled at that thought, happiness blooming inside of her. She carefully fixed up her resume, changing details, and adding in others where appropriate. She spent the better part of the day, sending it out to potential employers and recruiting agencies. While Alice enjoyed her current job, the amount of time she spent doing nothing was slowly driving her insane. She brought coffee and occasionally filed a document. Her office manager had a habit of micromanaging and eventually just took over every task himself. Alice had learned to shrug it off, but it was beginning to get on her nerves.

She had worked nearly as many jobs as there were weeks in the year, and each one had given her one thing or another to complain about. It was just the way things were. If it wasn't horrible hours, it was a ridiculous workload. However, she knew that despite the experience and potential for growth in her current position promised. She needed stability and better pay.

That is why she had applied just about everywhere, taking the time to write a cover letter for each company and position. When she had quit her first sales job for better prospects, Alice had been nervous and felt guilty. They had, after all, given her a chance to prove herself, and they had also offered to allow her to finish her schooling through them. Her boss pulled her aside and wished her the best of luck, reminding her, "Don't look for something you know; look for somewhere you can grow."

***

On Tuesday and Wednesday nights, Alice worked a shift at her local mom-and-pop pizza place. It wasn't glamorous, but it paid well in tips, especially since the clientele had come to know and recognize her. She had worked for the owners since she was sixteen, taking it as a second and often third job. She busted her ass and took as many shifts as she could safely handle, but often pushed herself to the point of exhaustion.

Alice had come home in the very early hours of the morning, the air chilly and her breath making small puffs of cloud as she exhaled. The local pizza place was one of the very last to stay open, often drawing in customers from many walks of life. Her favorite, of course, was the stoner college kid crowd that had the munchies and often hilarious and disastrous stories to share regarding their smoking experiences.

This usually meant that she only closed shop well after midnight. Alice also helped clean up and prep dough for the next day's business. It was tough work, but Alice had grown to like how busy she was while running the ovens.

"Alice."

Alice looked up from her hands, where she was fumbling with her keys. David's sudden appearance caused her to jump.

"What are you doing here, David?" Alice asked angrily, masking her sudden unease and the flood of desire. For all his faults, the man was good looking. His light hair was sticking out beneath his cap. His dark, smoldering eyes pierced her.

"We aren't done," he said, stepping towards her, gripping her arm tightly.

"Yeah, we are. Leave," Alice said, shrugging him off as she pushed past him to her door. Her body was tense, and she made a show of shoving her key in the lock, waiting for his departure.

"No, you threw a childish tantrum and left," David replied.

"You are not giving me any reason to stay with you right now, David," Alice said as she rolled her eyes, masking her fear as best she could, but her heart hammering. Would her neighbors hear her if she screamed?

"Come on, Alice. You and I both know you're going to come back to me anyway. Why not just do it sooner rather than later?" David said, his voice soothing and apologetic, coaxing and tugging at her desire to be wanted.

"David—" Alice started but then stopped herself.

"Baby, please. I'm sorry," David gently stroked his hand over her arm, and she stared at it.

Alice turned to him, "You're not here to make up. You're here for a booty call." Alice inhaled deeply through her nose, unable to quite process what was happening.

"Are you kidding me?" She said, fresh anger coursing through her veins.

David shrugged.

"Is that so bad? I mean, we were great together." She stared at him, horrorstruck. She turned the knob, kicking the door open, and grabbed his stuff, tossing the garbage bag at him.

"David, we're done. Go home," Alice turned around and swiftly slammed and locked the door behind her. She leaned her back against it, listening. She expected him to start hammering on her door, but it never came.

***

It was already late in the evening the following Friday when her phone's notification bell rang and startled her.

She sighed, dropping her head to her chest and groaning dramatically. Alice expected to open it to yet another message from David, groveling and pleading to have her back - either that or one that was littered with enough cussing to make Jonah Hill's eyes bleed.

She had been tempted to block David's number - even had her finger hovering over the button - but her curiosity had gotten the better of her. Alice wanted to see what other excuses, profanities, or stories he could dream up to text to her in his drunken stupors.

Whenever Alice thought of going back - whenever she felt like picking up her phone and calling him or asking him to come over - she just looked back at his messages, and the irritation drove her to reconsider. So far, it was working.

Alice's annoyance evaporated as soon as she unlocked her phone. It was a reply from Mercer Logistics, a major player in the tech business. Alice had done a brief search before applying for a position as a personal assistant. Quickly learning that Mercer Logistics had their hands in many different projects, nearly all of them making use of a program, they developed specifically to integrate with other service providers.

She carefully reread the email. Twice.

They wanted her for an interview first thing Monday. Alice squealed in happiness, hugging her phone to her chest and grinning from ear to ear. As soon as she caught her breath, another bout of squealing and rolling around got her flushed and winded.

She turned to her koala and buried her face in its soft fur.

"Everything's gonna change for us, Beanie."

Chapter 2

Alice could see the hesitation in Alexa Mercer's face. She knew that look well. Every interview she had had that week was a colossal disappointment. Many of them never went further than the perfunctory greeting and the standard interview questions that included asking her where she saw herself in five years. Alice knew she didn't fit the profile of the people they usually hired. She was sure that Alexa Mercer was humoring her for the mandated fifteen minutes before pulling the plug as well. Alice inhaled deeply and put on her bravest face. She had done a dozen interviews in the last week, but this one had given her butterflies.

"I'm sorry, Miss Dean. An issue has come up, and I have to ask that we reschedule our interview," Alexa Mercer said.

No. Alice felt her stomach drop.

"Don't look so worried," Alexa said.

"I'm still more than happy to meet with you. The timing of this is just bad."

"What if I came with you?" Alice blurted.

"We can have a mobile interview, and when we're done, I'll just take an Uber home or something."

Alice was mortified, but the words had already left her lips, and she could not play them off or take them back. The look Alexa gave her made Alice wish she could crawl in a hole and die.

She must think I'm—

"Alright," Alexa beamed.

"Perfect," Alice replied.

***

Alice peeked at Alexa every so often as they weaved through traffic. The woman looked incredible in a dusty gray power suit. The color complimented her skin tone, and Alice found herself staring at the longest legs that she had ever seen.

"If you could be an animal, what would it

be?" Alexa suddenly asked.

"I'm sorry, what?" Alice questioned.

"I don't ask standard interview questions, Miss Dean. I want to know who I'm hiring, and I want to know if they will be an asset to my company."

"I see." Her nerves were strung tight, and her throat had gone dry.

Alexa turned off onto a dirt road. The trip hadn't taken nearly as long as she had hoped, and Alice fidgeted with the hem of her blouse.

"I..." Alice slammed down on her nervous energy and decided to answer honestly.

"A butterfly," Alice answered.

Alexa glanced at the girl sitting in the passenger seat as she brought the SUV to a stop and waited, the vehicle still running. Alexa took her in. Her dark hair was carefully and meticulously straightened. Her eyes darted around, looking at everything but directly at Alexa. While she didn't demand full attention, Alexa at least expected some eye contact, regardless of the stress factor. The girl's long-sleeved blouse was buttoned up nearly to her chin. Alexa glanced down at the cuffs and made out a small shape peeking out that could only be part of a tattoo. Alice was inexperienced in Alexa's industry. Alexa had carefully gone over the girl's application and resume before her interview, phoning the references listed to try and get a feel for her. While she seemed likable enough, and her references had given her a standard good-kid-who-works-hard review, Alexa couldn't quite get a read on her.

Alexa had to force herself to reserve judgment, but it was hard. It had been her cover letter that had gotten her to agree to the interview in the first place.

"A grubby little worm can grow up to be…" Alice struggled to find the word, frowning at her carefully painted nails.

"Majestic," Alice said. Alexa said nothing.

"They seem weak only compared to other, bigger creatures," Alice said, "but they move differently like they're in a separate world. And to see them, you have to slow down, and sometimes, they surprise you, because you had no idea they were there all along," Alice said, not satisfied with her rambly, followed Alexa's lead, and became quiet.

A man approached the vehicle, waving at Alexa, one hand holding his hardhat in place as he jogged over, tie flapping over his shoulder.

"Let's go," Alexa said, unbuckling. She disembarked smoothly, her suit completely wrinkle-free.

Alice, however, had some trouble and nearly fell out of the SUV. Her foot had caught on the booster step just outside the door.

Alice stood slightly back, listening as Alexa and the site manager discussed the issues that had arisen. He handed each of them a hardhat and jogged away.

"Do you know what it is we're doing here?" Alexa asked as she donned the hat.

"I'm not a hundred percent on the lingo," Alice admitted, recalling the conversation between Alexa and the site manager.

"But I am eager and willing to learn," she

hastily added when she saw Alexa's shoulders draw up ever so slightly, a tenseness around her mouth and eyes.

"It sounds like somewhere along the chain, communication was dropped, and the container never made it to site. Without the materials, the technological—um, the infrastructure that is required to make the integration between the parent company and Mercer Logistics possible isn't in place. The site can't go live until the container gets here, right?" Alice didn't stop for a breath.

"It's not just importing and distribution of physical materials," she added.

"I also know that you developed the systems that the parent company will be using." Alice indicated the logo on the corner of the giant board announcing the new home of the business.

"It's what put Mercer Logistics on the map." Alice paused, feeling lightheaded. She had wanted to blow Alexa away and not make her regret requesting the interview. Alice knew she was inexperienced in this industry, but she needed someone to give her a break. It usually just takes one person.

"The main draw is usually the systems. The rest are just nice little extras. The clients will order stock and materials once, maybe twice, if you're lucky, but get them to sign on to the system integration, and you've got a client for years. They'll turn to you for any other system queries and often stick with the company even if there is unprepared downtime. Why? Because not many other businesses in the industry can do what you can." Alice wiped her hands on her black jeans and turned to face Alexa.

"Look, I know I'm a little out of my league here, but I am the right fit. I've been working since I was sixteen, and I have held so many jobs, working my ass off to get anywhere, and if I stuck out working three, horrible, unsafe, inhumane—"
She cut herself off, closed her eyes, and slowly, very carefully formed her last few sentences.

"I know that you built the company from the ground up, and even though you could probably have sold Mercer Logistics to the highest bidder and retired early, you stayed because you know what makes this place tick."

Alexa tilted her head and suppressed a smile.

Alice was smart, and she had shown a knack for stripping away the fluff to expose the baseline of information.

Alice paused again, gathered herself, and added, "I'm worth your time."

"Good girl," Alexa said, a smile finally breaking across her face. Alice stopped talking, her face flushed. The change was subtle, but it was noticeable. Alice had gone from this punk, almost-forceful, self-assured woman to a soft little girl.

Alice bit her lower lip, lowering her gaze to the floor, suppressing a smile. Her face was still burning. She shook her head slightly and lifted her gaze to Alexa's.

The wind caught Alice's hair and fanned it out, affording Alexa a flash of pink.

Alice's body tingled at the way Alexa looked at her. It was a combination of surprise and desire.

It caused a hot flush to pulse through her.

"We're done here," Alexa said, signing off on something and handed it over to the site manager who had appeared out of nowhere. She turned to Alice, taking in the demure, fragile expression on her face.

"I still have some questions for you, so if you've got the time, I'd like to continue our interview in a slightly more relaxed setting."
Her face lit up, and Alexa found herself pleased at the girl's response.

"Absolutely!"

***

After Alice left, Alexa's mind brought up that very innocent look on Alice's—her pink cheeks and the pleased smile on her face.
Her subtle submission had sent a thrill through Alexa. The girl's knowledge had surprised her.
Alexa shifted in her chair as she stared absentmindedly out of her office window. Alice had visibly relaxed when they were in a familiar

place. She had recommended a small coffee shop where the staff greeted her like she was a part of their family.

Full of surprises, Alice had offered to pay for their drinks and insisted on paying their server's tip even after the owner comped their coffee and pie.

She looked down at her desk, where Alexa had the potential candidates lined up next to one another. Alexa had been making notes on each of them before her mind had wandered. Alexa tapped the pen on the application she was on. It was Alice's. Along the margins were notes and memos to herself about how her interview had gone.

Alexa had already discarded many applications, and at first glance, Alice would have followed the same fate, but she had stood out more than the rest. She seemed to be a genuine and kind person. Alexa had noticed a slight shift in demeanor when her family and home life was brought up, but Alice had glossed over it and had tactfully diverted the topic.

Although her work experience came across as a tad excessive, Alexa appreciated that no matter where she had worked, she had stayed as long as it proved beneficial. She was torn between taking a chance on this little girl and going with someone certain to know what they were doing.

Yawning, Alexa switched her computer screen off and rolled her chair back in one smooth movement. It was already dark outside, long after everyone had already gone home for the day. She glanced back at the short stack of potential candidates. Her mind told her to choose the more mature, straight-laced lady that had experience in managing an office and running different departments.

On the other hand, there was Alice.

Alice was young and smart and had blown Alexa away at the site today. Usually, Alexa would sit on the decision for a few days to make sure she wasn't jumping the gun. She analyzed every aspect of every decision, but today her gut was telling her to throw her analytical side out the window and go with the girl.

John, Alexa's husband, continuously teased her about Alexa's inability to make snap decisions. He would almost always make huge, dramatic displays of exasperation when they were out together. She knew he was just teasing her goodnaturedly, and she loved that he was able to keep her grounded.

Alexa glanced at her watch, tapped her freshly manicured nail on the glass, and reached for the phone.

***

"May I please speak with Miss Dean?"

Alice sat up, nervous energy sparking inside of her.

"This is she."

"Miss Dean, this is Alexa Mercer."

"Oh," Alice's heart dropped a little, "How can I help?" She fiddled with Beanie in her lap, already bracing herself for the inevitable.

"I'd like you to come in tomorrow to go over some paperwork."

"Paperwork?" Alice questioned.

A soft, light laugh on the other line made her stomach clench unhappily.

"Does that mean..." Alice trailed off, hoping that Alexa would fill in the rest.

"Yes, Miss Dean. You've got the job."

Alice flopped back onto her bed after hanging up the phone, her ears still ringing. Did that happen?

"I thought I blew it," Alice said to herself, her mind reeling. She covered her face with a pillow and let out a squeal, kicking her legs. Alice hugged the pillow to her chest. She stared up at the ceiling, catching her breath and grinning from ear to ear.

Her mind then replayed the moment Alexa Mercer had called her a good girl. Then she thought about it again and again. She recalled the way her body had tingled and how easily she nearly slipped into her little space. There was this energy that Alexa Mercer gave off that simultaneously set her at ease and made her nervous. She was eager to please her. She wanted

Alexa to call her a good girl again, and Alice found herself imagining Alexa praising her as she satisfied her.

Chapter 3

Alice arrived to work before everyone else. She sat at her desk chair and waited, feeling out of her depth. Swiveling in her seat, she found the quiet to be slightly eerie. Alice hopped off to make some coffee and felt her pull-up shift uncomfortably beneath her skirt. Alice tried to wiggle it back into submission, but her it was sitting too tightly to move that way. She prepared the coffee machine and grimaced again as her pull-up pinched her skin. Alice hastily made her way to the bathroom, not wanting to take up too much time. She lifted her skirt and pinned the end of it under her chin as she shuffled the pull-up free and fixed her slip. She heard the coffee machine whistle a tune, and she hastily dropped her skirt, rushing from the bathroom.

Alexa half-glanced up from the document she had been poring over and paused as Alice appeared in front of her. Alexa turned her full attention to the girl.

She looked stunning in a frilled emerald green button-up blouse and a black skirt. Alexa let her eyes wander, and a smile spread to her lips. Alice's skirt was tucked into her pull-up. A rush of excitement flashed through her as she absently dropped the contract she was reading over onto the desk beside her and stepped closer to Alice.

"Here," she said. Alice looked up at Alexa, startled by how close she was standing.

"Wh—" Alice's face flushed a deep, hot red. Alexa had reached down and was gently tugging her skirt out of her pull-up. Alice felt embarrassment rise like a tidal wave inside of her. Alexa brushed her hand over Alice's rear, feeling the thicker material of the pull up beneath as she smoothed out the material of her skirt.

"There you go," Alexa said, giving Alice a knowing half-smile. She placed the softest of touches on Alice's cheek, "We don't want people to see your little secret."

Alice let out a surprised squeak and flushed a brighter scarlet.

"I won't tell if you don't," Alexa said, raising an eyebrow to the speechless Alice.

***

Alexa was positively thrilled at how subdued Alice was after their run-in outside of the bathroom. The subtle changes in her behavior belied her submissive nature. Alexa grinned as she remembered the pull-up. Little Alice certainly had surprised her.

Alice hadn't interacted with Alexa much after that, avoiding her gaze and furiously blushing when she caught Alexa staring. Alice busied herself with anything within reach to avoid catching Alexa's eye. Her body was still tingling from her touch. What had caught Alice by complete surprise wasn't that Alexa had seemed okay with seeing one of her employees in a pull-up, but rather that Alice had liked that it was her boss that had seen her.

"Alice," Alexa said, standing much too close to her, forcing the girl to look up at her through her.

Gosh, her eyes are gorgeous, Alexa thought to herself.

"Yes, Mrs. Mercer?"

"Call me Alexa," she said, her voice betraying her attraction. Alice swallowed.

"Yes, Alexa."

"Good girl," Alexa said, watching her face flush a second time.

"Did Thomas from accounting send the breakdown yet?"

"No, M— Alexa," Alice said, correcting herself. The approval on Alexa's face did something funny to her, as did her close presence. Alice could feel her arousal pool between her legs each time Alexa looked at her.

"Get him up here for me, won't you?"

"Yes, Alexa."

"Perfect, and when you're done with that, come see me in my office," Alexa said. Alice's heart stalled.

"Deep breath, Alice. You're not in trouble." Alexa saw the immediate relief on her face and suppressed a smile.

Alice is such a baby, Alexa thought.

"I want to show you how to begin managing my day-to-day as soon as possible," Alex explained. Alice nodded, "Is there anything else you need?" Alice softly asked. Alexa thought for a moment.

"Not right now, you've been such a good girl," Alexa cooed. Alice, feeling a head-spinning arousal build inside of her.

Chapter 4

"John," Alexa said. The tone of her voice drew his attention immediately. He looked up from his guitar, the pick still between his teeth, to look at her. His brow was furrowed in concern. He carefully set his instrument down and removed the pick.

"John. You wouldn't believe how adorable the new girl is," Alexa gushed.

"Annie?"

"Alice," Alexa corrected.

"She blew me away in the interview, and today, oh my gosh."
John smiled, curious, leaning forward in his seat, "What on Earth happened?"

"She wore a pull-up."

"What?" John's voice was louder than he had intended.

"Yes!"

"There was just this vibe, you know?" Alexa said.

"She had a wardrobe malfunction, and I reached down and helped her."

John watched as his wife's face glowed. She started describing how distracting it had been after she had fixed little Alice's pull-up.

"She was so different after that - so demure - and her blushing cheeks were too cute not to touch," Alexa sighed deeply and grinned.

"I think you'd love her, John."

"Really?"

"I think she has an Instagram account," Alexa said, excited to share her find with her husband. She bounced up off the couch to fetch her tablet from the home office. John shook his head and smiled.

"She must be something special for you to go on about her like this."

Alexa returned with her tablet in hand, her eyes glittering with wild excitement, "She's perfect; smart and cute, and..." Alexa paused as she clicked on Alice's profile.

"See."

The girl was stunning. Her chocolate brown hair

hung straight past her shoulders, her equally alluring eyes staring right through him. Her lips were small but full, and her smile promised him wonder-filled days.

"Wow," he breathed.

They scrolled through her posts, landing on one where she was dressed in a white onesie, posing cutely for the camera. Her breasts were perfect for her slight build. He admired the tropical tattoos on her thigh. Alice's pose reminded him of a little girl caught doing naughty things, and it stirred heat through him. John lifted Alexa easily, setting her on his lap, her back to his chest, "Did she turn you on?" John felt her squirm, a slow smile spreading across his face.

"Tell me what you want to do to her, Alexa," John murmured in her ear. Her body was pressed against him, and he could feel himself grow hard. He ran his hands over her front, unbuttoning her blouse.

Alexa inhaled sharply, her body tingling. She bit her lip as she eyed the picture on her screen, glancing over her shoulder at him. She recognized the light in his eyes, and it sent a shiver through her.

He unclasped the front catch of her bra and lightly bit her ear, growling. His wife's breathing changed, and he felt her nipples grow hard beneath his touch.

"Tell me," he demanded.

"I want her to call me, Mommy," Alexa moaned. John slowly slid his hand down her smooth belly, dipping his hand below the waistband of her skirt.

"Do you want her to touch you?" John asked, stroking the soft skin above the elastic of her underwear.

"Yes," she said breathlessly.

"I want you to touch her," John whispered.

"While you watch?" Alexa's face turned a delicious shade of pink as she thought it over. Her mind wandered to the look on Alice's face when Alexa had sensually pressed herself against the girl while pulling her pull-up into place.

"What if she offered to please her, Daddy?

Would you just watch then?" Alexa groaned and gyrated against him.

"Do you want her to suck on your nipples?" John asked, pinching her nipple, eliciting a moan from her.

"Just imagine bathing her, running a washcloth over that pale, soft skin of hers," John whispered, running his tongue over Alexa's earlobe. Alexa's skirt rode up as she straddled him, grinding against his swelling cock, exposing the warm, caramel skin of her thighs. John's eyes landed on the lace of her underwear, and he felt his cock jerk.

He pulled his hand free and stroked her thighs.

"Imagine little Alice standing for you to rub lotion onto her skin after a bath."

Alexa leaned back into him, running the palm of her hand over his bulge, her cheeks flushed, and her nipples hard.

"I want you, John." His erection pressed uncomfortably against the zipper of his jeans. He gripped her by the waist, pressing himself against her core, delighting in the soft moan that escaped.

"Right here?" John asked, his voice hoarse. Alexa nodded, her mind swirling. He slid the back of his hand over her mound, moisture already making her panties stick to her swollen lips. He pressed a fingertip against her, massaging her clit. Alexa bit back a moan, leaning her head back.

"Imagine little Alice touching you like this," John said. Alexa moaned again, and he grinned. John slipped his fingertips beneath the elastic of her panties, and his wife shuddered. He teased her, stroking the skin around the edges of her underwear, chills erupting over her skin.

"Imagine little Alice on her knees in front of you, her tongue trailing up your thigh to your pussy."

"Why are you teasing me?" Alexa moaned, the rough, calloused fingers sending shivers through her, her body burning for more of his touch.

"I want you to beg," John said, pulling her closer with his free hand, planting kisses along the nape of her neck. Goosebumps exploded over her skin, and Alexa moaned loudly, grinding against his hand.

"I want you to imagine teaching little Alice how to please me."

He held her waist, keeping her still as Alexa growled at him, "Stop teasing me."

Alexa saw the glint in his eyes and the smirk that spread across his face at her words. Alexa fought against his hold, needing his touch to soothe her.

"No, no," John said grinning.

Frustrated, Alexa pressed herself against him, hovering her lips over his. She felt him stiffen as his fingers dug into her soft flesh.

"I can tease, too," Alexa whispered, her lips still barely touching his.

John's cock pulsed, and his breathing became heavy. Alexa knew exactly what drove him insane, and he loved it.

"Careful, Alexa."

Alexa leaned back so he could see her face. She pulled her bottom lip between her teeth and tilted her head in a cutesy way, challenging him to resist. She leaned forward again and flicked her tongue over his bottom lip.

It got the response she had wanted. John groaned and pressed his groin against hers, his hands holding her tightly against him as he thrust against her. His response sent a wave of pleasure coursing through her veins. His urgency ignited her, and a flashfire of hot need tore through her. Alexa grinned, her eyes flashing at him.

John stood, his strong arms bulging as he lifted Alexa effortlessly. With one hand, he held her to him, and with the other, he unbuttoned and unzipped his jeans, freeing his rock-hard cock. He shoved her panties aside and lowered her down, her moist, warm pussy gripping him tightly as he pushed into her.

Alexa inhaled as she took his full length into her, feeling his hardness fill her up. All thoughts of teasing him had dissolved in desire. Alexa pressed her lips against his and suckled on his lower lip, begging for more.

John groaned at the taste of her, his cock hard

and throbbing, pleasure guiding his slow thrusts as he pushed himself deeper into his wife.

Alexa's moans spurred him on, and he felt a familiar tightening of his balls. He pulled out, wanting to make their encounter last as long as possible.

"No," Alexa whimpered as he pulled away.

"Relax, my love. We're not done yet."

"What are you doing?" He set her down on the couch, pushing her skirt up to her belly and pulling her panties down.

Alexa gasped as the cold leather of the couch, touched the bare skin of her ass. John stuffed her underwear into the pocket of his jeans and spread her legs wide.

"I want you to scream my name," John said as he lowered his face to her pussy, his tongue flicking over her clit.

"I want you to imagine little Alice doing this to you."

Alexa's body twitched, and a whimper escaped her lips.

"Imagine her pleasing her, Mommy.

Imagine her being pleased just like this."

Her body was flushed, tingling. Her mind a whirl of thoughts of John and Alice.

"John," Alexa breathed, her eyes unable to focus. She grasped the backrest of the couch for support.

"Tell me what you want, Alexa," John said, his fingers slowly circling her dripping core, his thumb massaging her clit. He pushed a finger inside of her, drawing a soft moan from her lips. He inserted one more and drew yet another moan from her lips. Alexa arched her back.

"John, I want you."

He brought his lips to her moist folds and suckled on her, flicking his tongue over her clit. Her scent was making cum drip from the head of his cock, but he held back. He wanted Alexa to ask for it.

"I need your cock," Alexa said, her moan turning into a heavy whimper.

"Where do you need it?"

"I want your throbbing cock inside of my pussy, John. I want you to fuck me."

John's cock jerked violently, and he had to clench his jaw to keep from cumming. He continued to massage his wife's clit as he pressed the head of his cock against her opening. Alexa let out a low growl of anticipation.

He pushed his cock into her moist heat, and Alexa's body clenched around him, pulsing lightly as she edged her orgasm.

"Oh, yes," Alexa moaned.

"Don't you dare cum yet, Alexa." He draped himself over her, drinking in her scent, planting kisses against her neck and cheek as she met his slow thrusts, quivering beneath him.

"I love you," Alexa whispered into his ear as she gently scraped her nails down his back. She felt John's cock throb once, and he had to slow his thrusts to keep himself controlled.

"I love you," he said, rubbing his face in her neck.

He gently bit down on her shoulder, and she panted.

Their bodies were warm, glittering with a fine sheen of sweat and sex as they rocked together.

His cock swelled, and he growled in her ear, "Cum for me. I want to feel it on my cock." Alexa bit down on a loud moan as her body exploded around his cock. Her pussy clenched tightly, pulsing around him, milking him as he continued to draw her orgasm out.

John pulled out, slowly, watching as bliss and pleasure played across her face.

"How was that, Mommy?" John winked at her.

"I've got so much more planned, Alexa," John whispered, massaging her breasts, running his thumbs over her nipples.

John and Alexa laid on the bed in the dark, panting, and still entwined. Alexa pressed her face into his neck and inhaled his scent and heat. Her body was still twitching and thrumming.

"Fuck." Alexa laughed.

"Want to do that again?" Alexa asked. She raised her eyebrows at him, her hand already scraping along the dusting of dark, prickly hair running from his navel to the base of his cock before stroking him again.

***

Alice dropped her bag on the kitchen counter and kicked her shoes off. Her body was wired. She had been begging to be touched all day. After the incident with Alexa, Alice had found it hard to concentrate on her work, stealing glances at Alexa whenever she stopped by. She recalled the way Alexa's hands felt on her skin as she helped fix her skirt. She remembered the hungry look in her eyes when she called her 'little Alice.' Alice's heart thumped wildly. She grabbed her laptop and set it on the edge of her bed, waiting for it to boot up as she stripped off her work clothes and walked around her apartment naked. Her work clothes were so restrictive.

She opened the link and stared. Her personal Instagram had nearly a thousand posts. Alice scrolled through them, admiring the beauty of each shot. Alice leaned forward and looked at the photo of Alexa with her husband, reading that his name was John. She paused at one where

John was looking straight at the camera, guitar in hand. His dusty blonde hair was hanging over one side of his face, and there was a guitar pick between his teeth. A tremor went through her body. He was hot, and Alice licked her lips her, recognizing him. She had been to most of his local performances, delighting in the way the music had made her feel and losing herself in the lyrics. Alice spent some time going through his photos, each one highlighting his form. She felt moisture pool between her legs while at the same time, a hot vibration shuddered through her core. There was one where he and his wife were lying in bed, hair mussed, sheets hinting at their naked forms beneath. Alice's hand slipped between her legs, absently running her fingers over her swollen mound, moistening her panties. Alice opened Alexa's account, and her heart hammered in her chest. The woman had a body to die for. Her account showed posts of her everyday life, from having coffee in bed with John to sitting poolside in the smallest bikini known to man, showing off every dip and curve.

The next one had Alexa dressed in nothing but a slightly-too-big leather jacket and aviator sunglasses. Alice moaned out loud when she read a caption on the photo: Mommy knows you've been bad, baby.

Chapter 5

"Rats," Alice muttered, shaking the contents of her purse out onto her desk.

"What?" Alexa asked, her eyes skimming over a document as she walked up behind her.

"Oh, it's nothing," Alice said, hastily trying to shove her things back into the empty bag. Alexa eyed the mess and arched her brow.

"I forgot my wallet," Alice relented, and she laughed at her little slip-up.

"I guess that's what I get for going to bed at three in the morning."

"What were you doing up so late?" Alexa asked. Alice managed to hide the fact that her cheeks had turned pink by faking a coughing fit.

"Just Netflix," Alice mumbled. She took a drink of water.

"Lunch is on me," Alexa said.

"What, no. I can't."

"Can't eat?" Alexa asked grinning. She pulled a couple of fifties from her pocket and stuffed them into Alice's hands before she could protest further.

"Thanks," Alice said, taken back by Alexa's generosity.

"A good little girl would get a spanking for leaving something so important at home," Alexa murmured and held on to her. Alice's eyes grew wide, and she took the smallest of steps back, her heart beginning to race.

"You want Mommy to spank you, Alice?" Alexa asked, pressing herself closer to her. Alexa could feel herself getting aroused. The blush on Alice's face certainly didn't help the situation.

"I can promise you that punishment would be in order if you were my little girl," Alexa murmured. Alice moaned, quivering at the thought, her knees weakening. Alice didn't know if Alexa had put her arms around her, and that was why her knees gave out or if Alexa had caught her. There was an unmistakable glint of lust in Alexa's gaze as she breathed into her ear.

"Just imagine me pulling you over my lap and spanking you for being a naughty girl." Alice licked her lips as she stared into Alexa's eyes. Alexa leaned in ever so slightly.

"Alexa, call for you on line three," a boxy, scratchy voice announced, breaking the tension. Annoyed, Alexa reached past Alice and pressed the button on the intercom. Without breaking eye contact with Alice, she asked, "Who is it?"

"Geoff from DigiTech," the voice replied.

"Fine, I'll shift some meetings. Put him through to my office," Alexa said.

"Yes, Alexa."

"Get yourself a little treat too, Alice." Alice stared at Alexa's lips, feeling her belly do a little flip when she said her name.

***

Alice's eyes kept drifting over to Alexa. She was on the phone with a supplier. Her hair pulled into a neat bun instead of the loose locks they had been this morning. Alice dropped her gaze to Alexa's breasts, and thoughts of her suckling on them came unbidden to her. Alice chewed on her lip as she imagined her tongue flicking over her boss' nipples, sucking them. She shifted in her seat, pressing her thighs together, trying to lessen the pressure between her legs. Her mind drifted to John and Alexa together, and her face flushed a bright scarlet. Alexa caught her gaze and smirked. Alice hastily looked away from her, her heart pounding. She kept replaying Alexa's words in her mind, loving the way Alexa had called herself Mommy. Alice allowed herself to think about what it would be like to have Alexa as her Mommy and to have Alexa help her change into her onesie after a nice warm bath.

"Distracted?" Alexa asked from right behind her. Alice jumped a little in her seat, "No. Of course not." Alexa saw color streak across her cheeks, turning her ears bright red. She grinned, "Of course not." Alexa pressed her legs against Alice's, delighting in the warmth of her skin, "You wouldn't want to get into trouble again, would you?" She looked up at Alexa, her height and heels forcing her to tilt her head back. Alice shook her head ever so slightly, her big submissive eyes making Alexa's heart pound.

"Good," Alexa said, stepping away from her, continuing on her way to yet another meeting as if nothing had just transpired between them.

***

Alice leaned against her apartment door, keys still in hand.

"Oh, gosh." Alice giggled, then burst out laughing.

"I'm so screwed." Alice slid down to the floor, still laughing, her heart thumping wildly inside her chest. When her hysterics died down, Alice got to her feet.

"I am so screwed." Her mind wandered again to an image of Alexa as she leaned on her desk, sensually rubbing her thighs together as she talked to her husband over the phone. She could swear that Alexa's touch lingered on Alice's skin.

Her body tingled, reminding her of the way Alexa

had made her feel, reminding her of the fact that she'd been soaking through her panties all day. Alice absentmindedly unbuttoned her blouse, the cool air causing her nipples to harden beneath her bra. Her mind recalled the incident with Alexa at lunch.

Good girl. Alice imagined Alexa was right there with her.

Mommy knows you've been bad, baby girl.

She rubbed her clit, her eyes locked on Alexa's as she imagined her pulling her over her lap, spanking her for staying up past her bedtime. Her legs were shaking. Alice closed her eyes and imagined the feel of Alexa's breasts against her bare skin. She slipped her fingers past her panties and slowly pushed them inside her.

Are you going to be a naughty little girl again? You know naughty little girls get punished.

Alice's breathing sped up, her orgasm drawing closer as Alexa's words echoed in her head. Alice's body tightened around her fingers, and sparks exploded behind her lids as she came, hard. She stayed where she was, her fingers still inside her core, letting that floaty feeling wash over her.

"Yep. Definitely screwed."

Chapter 6

"Miss Dean? Are you still there?" Came the man's voice down the phone. Alice felt the blood rush to her head while it pounded painfully in her ears and behind her eyes. Her throat tightened, and her heart was racing.

"Yes," Alice choked out.

"Do you have someone who can drive you?" The voice asked.

"Um," Alice blinked slowly and stupidly. Her heart was torn in two directions, and it made her stomach swirl nauseatingly.

"What's the address? I'll be there soon," Alice replied.

***

The unpleasantness of everything was overwhelming. Alice felt dizzy as she waited outside the morgue. She buried everything—the fresh wave of emotion that came when she'd gotten the call, everything. It was too much. She had numbed herself to all that was around her, building a wall, feeling muted and blocked off.

And when she stood over them, she felt nothing. Alice knew that she would feel guilty about it later, but at that moment, there was nothing.

"It's them," Alice confirmed with the coroner.

"Where—" She caught herself, "No, I'd rather not know." The man nodded and filled out the paperwork. Alice left the room, clutching her keys so tightly that they cut painfully into her hand.

***

Alice kept wiping her hands on her jeans, her fingertips cold, and her head hurting from tension. She wiped her hands another time and compared the address to the one she had saved on her phone.

She remained in her car, just staring at the faded blue door that set their house apart from the matchboxes beside it. Alice forced herself to turn off the car and get out. Otherwise, she would be there all night.

At first, she just stood on the sidewalk staring at the small, unassuming house that lay between similarly modest and dingy-looking houses. Then she took small, shaky steps toward it. The distance between the sidewalk and the front door stretched out further with each step, feeling like hours had passed, until, suddenly, reality snapped back into place, and she found herself standing right in front of the door much sooner than she had wished. Alice hesitated on the threshold. The house seemed to grow taller and scarier, looming over her. She had been on her own since she was sixteen. She hadn't expected the place to be still standing ten years after the fact. Alice hadn't been back since the night her mom had screeched at her to get out. A cold sweat broke out on her back as she unlocked the door to the small rental house. She slowly pushed it open. It was like walking through a door to the past. Memories assaulted her, and she wiped her palms on her jeans over and over again, no longer feeling anything but the burn in her stomach.

I wish I got rid of you like my Mom had wanted me to!

Her mom's voice repeated in her mind, the pain echoing dully. Her dad had been too high to care. To be fair, it was a normal state for both of them, but that night, Lena had thrown ashtrays and other objects at her. Glass and ceramics had shattered around her. Alice blinked. Nothing had changed except, perhaps, the fact that less personal things and more trash were lying around than she remembered. The divot in the wall was still there where the second ashtray had sailed over her head the night she had left.

"You can do this," Alice said to herself as she fought with a stack of flattened boxes. The silence in the house caused an unpleasant chill to travel through her.

It smelled stale. Another memory assailed her. She recalled coming home from school with a friend and finding her mom so coked up that she just stared blankly at them, gently rocking herself where she sat on the kitchen floor, drooling on herself. It was also the last time she had invited a friend over.

***

The last room was hers. When Alice had left home, she had taken only a small handful of things. Alice was surprised to see that they had left her space virtually untouched. Virtually, because anything of value had been stripped and sold off, no doubt for money to fund their habits or to pay rent, but the rest had been left in, more or less, the same place.

She couldn't breathe due to pressure in her chest. Alice forced one foot in front of the other as she entered deeper into the room. There was a distinct smell of old, stale air and smoke that had filtered and soaked into everything. Alice dragged an empty box into the room behind her and stood idly in the center, her mind a whirl of emotions and flashes of memories. She felt a strange, familiar echoing emptiness, and she found herself looking down at her body in that room, automatically beginning the process of clearing it out. She folded the ratty bedding and shook the dust from a pillow. She then stuffed them into a trash bag. She would donate these, she thought. Other small knick-knacks that were worthless to her parents had gathered a layer of dust and discolored the wood and plastic. There was a little wooden bird her dad had carved for her when she was three. The wood was dry and cracked. She picked it up carefully. The wood was rough beneath her fingertips, and she had a memory of her dad pointing out bright red plumage of the robin he was copying. She had giggled happily, squealing and shaking her already-thin arms. A vicious reminder invaded her mind. There may have been sweet moments interspersed with the bad, but this had never been her home. They hadn't wanted her. Alice grew angry, and her hand tightened around the small figurine.

"Just throw it away," she said to the

empty room.

"I should just throw it all away."
Alice leaned her head against her knees and whispered to herself, "Why am I even here?" She looked again at the small bird and squashed the impulse to destroy it. She carefully placed it at the top of the box with a handful of other odds and ends, and then she taped it shut. Her clothes wouldn't fit her anymore, so she opted to donate those, too. Alice cleaned up her room much faster than she had anticipated. There hadn't been much of her left in that place, anyway. Alice struggled and tilted the bed onto its side, upsetting a couple of daddy long leg spiders as they wobbled away, hastily over the dusty carpet. She gathered the scraps of paper, stray socks, and clumps of dust bunnies. She gave the room a good once-over, making sure that everything had been packed up. The curtains were faded and just as dusty as everything else in the room. She would take those down after running a vacuum through the place. She vaguely considered getting a service to come out and clean the hole

for her, but Alice knew that even had she been paid, she couldn't afford to spend frivolously.

Alice had separated everything that she was going to donate from the things she could sell or would keep. The rest of the boxes were stacked neatly up against the wall by the front door. There hadn't been very much to clear out, but it still amounted to a couple of boxes of keepsakes, junk, and various items, books, and stacks of yellowed photos she couldn't bear to sort through yet. She did call a service to collect the things she was going to donate. They collected for free, and since they hailed from the area, the trip wouldn't cost them very much in terms of fuel. Alice helped the older man load the things into his truck.

"Thank you for collecting these things, sir," she said numbly.

"Thank you for donating them to us, missy. As you know, we are more than happy to take them." Alice took her last $50 from her pocket and handed it to him after everything was loaded. She had given them the mattresses as well, sure that someone else could make better use of them than she could.

"You've given so much, miss," the old man said, his eyes wide. No doubt, he had taken in the general look of the neighborhood and had drawn his conclusions regarding her financial situation. While it was true that she wasn't living quite as comfortably as she wanted, she wasn't living the way she had growing up in this house. Alice no longer went to bed hungry.

"Please, it's not much, but I want you to have it."

His old eyes softened, and he wrapped his warm wrinkled hands around hers, thanking her again, taking the offering.

She didn't wait for him to leave before returning to the house. She loaded the boxes in her car and went back inside, standing in the empty living room/kitchen. The sun was already setting, a chill creeping into the house. Alice had briefly considered sleeping in there, but she had already broken her promise of never returning. She wasn't about to fall asleep in a house she hated, surrounded by memories that would choke her to death while she slept.

After some deliberation, Alice spent the night sleeping upright in her car.

She spent the greater majority of the weekend packing, cleaning, and dealing with the legal paperwork and meetings that were required in situations such as hers. She had them cremated but didn't bother picking them up from the funeral home. She drove home in the dark, not once glancing back at the darkened windows of her parents' crappy house.

***

"Morning, Alice," Alexa said, smiling brightly. Alice smiled, the action feeling hollow and rehearsed, "Morning, Alexa." If Alexa had noticed the lack of warmth in her tone, she didn't acknowledge it. Alice watched her walk into her office and close the door behind her.

Good, Alice thought. She wouldn't be able to force a smile or convince anyone she was okay for too long. Remaining numb was what was keeping her upright at the moment, and the less she thought and felt, the better.

Before lunch, Alexa buzzed her, "Alice, could you please bring me DigiTech's file?"

"Here, Alexa." Alice said as she entered after a quick, soft knock.

"Is there anything else?" Alice asked. Alexa looked at her, and Alice felt her gaze bore through her much like she had that first day they met.

"Is there something on your mind?" Alexa asked tentatively.

"If you're not happy with the work, we can figure something out."
Alice shook her head, "The work is great, Alexa, really..." She stopped herself, feeling the familiar tightness in her throat. She forced a smile, "I'm just a little tired. I didn't sleep well." It wasn't entirely a lie. Alexa didn't press. Alice was entitled to her privacy.

"I'll have Gabe order us something from

the Greek deli down the street. They have the best coffee." Alexa offered. Alice nodded, the fake smile still on her lips, "That sounds great. Thank you, Alexa."

***

Alexa watched her carefully as she stirred sugar into her coffee. It was too much for her taste, but she knew that Alice had a liking for sweet things. Her instinct was to hold Alice's smaller frame in her arms and rock her until she fell asleep. She felt a tug inside her heart and kept trying to connect to Alice, but Alice wasn't letting her in. Alexa didn't want to let her go home tonight if she wasn't sure of her mental state.

"How was your weekend, Alice? Didn't you say you were going to go out with some friends?" Alexa probed, watching her face closely. The smile dropped away, and the cup lowered from her face.

"I..." Alice's voice grew thick, and she cleared her throat. "I was..."

"Alice?" Alexa asked, leaning forward, "Are you okay?" Alice felt the wave of tears rise and break over her. They welled up inside her, obscuring her vision, and choking her.

"I'm..." Fine. The word died in her throat, and she swallowed against the tightness in her chest. She felt as if she was going to vibrate apart.

"Would it be okay if I hugged you?" Alexa asked. Alice's body was shaking, but in a fragile state of mind, even the kindest touch could cause mental and physical distress if the person did not want to be touched. Alice nodded. The moment Alexa's arms wrapped around her, she lost her composure. She buried her head against Alexa's shoulder and cried. Everything she had held in over the last ten years, ever since she left that house, came out in one great flood. She sobbed, shaking, and unable to breathe through the tears and the screams.

"Shh, it's okay," Alexa said, stroking her hair. She could feel Alice's tears soak into her shirt, but Alexa didn't care. When Alice's sobs finally quieted, she looked at Alexa apologetically.

"Here," Alexa said, handing her a makeup wipe and several tissues.

"I'm sorry. I didn't mean to just fall apart like that."

"Don't be, Alice," Alexa said and patted her arm, "We need to let our emotions out, or they'll hide in our hearts until we shatter." Alice cleaned herself up, using Alexa's compact mirror to make sure the streaks of mascara and eyeliner were cleanly wiped away.

"So, tell me what happened, Alice. Please. I want to help," Alexa almost begged. Alice nodded, drying her eyes.

"My parents died over the weekend." Alice didn't know how to finish her thought, "I hadn't been back there since I was sixteen."

"I take it you didn't have the best relationship with them?" Alexa questioned. Alice shook her head.

"Do you have other family?" Alexa looked at Alice with compassion.

"My aunt, but she wasn't on speaking terms with my mom. I was the only one they could reach." She dropped her head in her hands and sighed, pulling her fingers through her hair as she looked at Alexa.

"Come on," Alexa said, holding her hand out to Alice.

"I think we should get out of here. Get you home."

Alice shook her head, her eyes finding the pattern on the carpet beneath her feet.

"You can't stay here all night, Alice," Alexa said, her voice firm but kind.

Alice looked up at her, surprised at how easily she allowed Alexa to take control.

Alexa called one of the clerks into her office.

"Please arrange that Miss Dean's vehicle is delivered to her residence. I'm taking her home."

"Yes, Mrs. Mercer."

Alexa held her hand out to Alice again, a soft smile on her face.

"Please?" Alice hesitantly took it.

"Thank you, Alexa," Alice whispered.

****

"Buckle your seatbelt, please," Alexa said. Alice's hands were shaking too much, "I..." She stopped, feeling her instinctual response to keep her little side hidden. The stress was too much, and she could feel her brain clench tightly in response. Alice didn't want to go home. Alice looked at Alexa with new tears in her eyes, pleading silently.

"Here," Alexa said, leaning over and clipping the buckle in place. Alexa's flowery scent filled her nose, and she whispered a small thank you.

"Where do you live?" Alexa asked. Alice shook her head.

"I don't want to go home. I can't." She remembered the unpacked boxes waiting for her when she did eventually get there. She shook her head again, more firmly than before.

"Then I'm taking you home with me," Alexa said, settling the matter.

"I don't think you should be alone, anyway." Alice nodded. They spent the ride home in silence, Alice feeling her mind pull back from her emotions again, too tired to talk or think.

***

"Drink your tea, sweetie," Alexa said kindly, "It'll warm you up." Alice automatically did as she was told; her eyes still red from tears. She had felt embarrassed at first, having broken down in front of her boss, but Alexa didn't seem to mind it at all. Alexa was kind and caring and had let her be.

"Good girl," Alexa said with a smile. Alice felt her heart thump once, and new tears threatened to fall.

"Do you want to talk about it?" John asked, his gray eyes warm. He touched her cheek, wiping away a stray tear. It was a nice type of weird to be meeting John amidst her most vulnerable place. Alice shook her head.

Then, after a few moments, she nodded.

"I don't know." Her voice cracked, becoming softer.

"It's okay," John said. He looked at his wife.

"Alexa and I—we're here for you. Whatever you need. We'll take care of you, okay?" Alice wished in her heart that it was true, and when she met their gazes, she believed them. There was not a single trace of judgment or disgust coming from them.

"Promise?" Alice asked, her voice light and small, tears spilling over again.

"Promise," John said. Alice threw her arms around him and sobbed for the second time in less than an hour. Alexa smiled, her heart warmed by the sight of John's tenderness as he stroked Alice's hair and let her tears soak through his favorite shirt.

"I'll run you a nice warm bath, Alice. Would you like that?" John asked her. Alice nodded, still sobbing.

"Come with me," Alexa said, leading Alice

to the master bedroom and en-suite bathroom. Alice was barely able to take in the design and beauty of the place. Her head was fuzzy, and her eyes burned. Alexa's hand was wrapped around hers, and she stared down at it. She was shaking, scared, and sad. Alice wished she didn't have these feelings for her parents. She hated them, and she loved them, and she wished that her life had been different from the start. When Alice just stood numbly in front of the bubble-filled tub, Alexa touched her hand again, drawing her attention.

"Can you stay with me?" Alice asked.

"Of course, Alie."

Alice's heart jumped happily at the little nickname Alexa had given her. She'd always just been Alice. Alice hesitated, her fingers hovering over the buttons on her blouse and then fumbling with the buttons.

"Do you want me to help?" Alexa asked, patiently waiting for Alice to answer.

With more tears, Alice replied, "Yes."

"Yes, please," Alexa said, gently stressing

the addition. Alice looked at her. There was no malice or anger in her words or face and it made Alice smile.

"Yes, please," Alice repeated, dropping her hands to her side. Alice inhaled a shaky breath, Alexa's light floral perfume mingling with the fruity scent of the bubble bath she had used. Alexa smiled reassuringly at Alice and quickly unbuttoned her blouse, tugging on the edges to free it from her skirt. She carefully folded it and placed it on the counter. Alexa then tucked her thumbs into the elastic of Alice's flower-print, ankle-length skirt and gently tugged it down over her hips. The lacy underwear threw Alexa for a brief moment. It was sensual and matched her bra, the black material contrasting her pale skin. Alexa swallowed, trying to steady her hands. It was the first time she touched Alice's body. Alice stepped out of the skirt, placing her hand on Alexa's shoulders for a little support. She felt goosebumps kiss her skin as the cool air flowed over her from the open doorway. Alexa took in the girl's body. Various colorful tattoos were covering her right arm and several large tropical flowers on her thigh. She made a note to ask her about them later. Right now, Alexa just wanted to get her warm and comfortable and let her be. Alexa reached around her, unclasping her bra. Alice's breasts bobbed free, and Alexa took a moment to admire the perkiness of her small breasts. Alice stepped out of her underwear as well. She hadn't worn her pull-up today. Her brain had been a tired mess when she'd woken up this morning, so she had left just about everything at home.

"I'll wash these for you," Alexa said, carefully placing Alice's things in a neat little pile on the countertop. Alice nodded.

"Hey, love," John called from the bedroom, standing just outside the doorway to afford them some privacy. Alice instinctively covered herself, her face flushing a deep scarlet.

"Yeah?" Alexa answered.

"I've left some things on the bed that Alice can wear for the night. I thought she might like something a little more comfortable to wear."

"What a great idea!" Alexa said. She turned to Alice. "Are you okay with that?"
She nodded.

"Thank you," Alice whispered. Alexa looked at her big, trusting eyes and smiled.

"Anything, Alice. I mean it."

"Why are you so nice to me?" Alice blurted.

"Aren't you weirded out by me? By my voice, by my crying, my neediness, and by me being a little?" Tears rolled down her cheeks.
Alexa smiled again, "You needed someone to take care of you, Alie." Alice pouted, "Yeah, but—"

"You're perfect the way you are, Alice. Come. Let's get you cleaned up so you can wear something cute and warm." Alexa smiled, interrupting her.
Alice carefully dipped a foot into the tub, testing the water with her toes. She giggled as the bubbles tickled her foot as she lowered it in.

"How's the water? Do you need me to add some cold in?" Alexa asked.

"No, it's perfect," Alice said.

"Thank you," she added, almost forgetting her manners again. Alice stepped into the tub and lowered herself to the water. The peach scent of the bubble bath enveloped her, and Alice exhaled a pent-up breath. Her tears had finally dried up. The last few weeks of her life had gone completely unhinged.

"I thought you might like this," Alexa said and handed her a rubber duck that was dressed up like a unicorn. Alice giggled again, hastily reaching out to grab it, but then caught herself. Alexa didn't seem to mind her childlike behavior. It seemed to Alice that Alexa approved that she was so relaxed around her and John.

"It's okay, Alie."

Alice gently took the ducky and thanked her, letting it float between a mountain of peach-scented bubbles. Alexa made herself comfortable on the bathroom floor while Alice slowly warmed up, becoming a little more talkative as the bubbles and warm water did their magic.

"Remember to wash between your toes

too, Alie," Alexa said as she watched Alice squeeze a dollop of shower gel onto a sponge.

"Yes, Mommy," Alice said.

There was a heartbeat of stillness when Alice's words left her lips. Her eyes grew wide, and she paused, foam dripping from the sponge into the water. She hadn't meant for the word to come out, but it had. Horror washed over her, and she stared, unblinking, at the water.

"Good girl," Alexa said, not missing a beat. She could tell that Alice was used to having to keep her little self hidden away from people around her. She wondered if Alice had ever had a Caregiver - not just some relationship that had a little kindness to it, but a real caregiver.

Alice peeked at Alexa from the corner of her eye as she started washing. The woman was relaxed, sitting cross-legged and watching over Alice as she washed and played with the unicorn ducky.

"Mommy?" Alice asked, testing the word again, feeling self-conscious.

"Yes, Alie?"

"Can I have soup for dinner?" Alexa

arched a brow.

"Please?" Alice amended, blushing.

"We'll see what we can scrounge up, baby girl." Alice got out of the tub, and Alexa wrapped her in the biggest, fluffiest, and warmest towel she had ever seen or touched in her entire life. She ran her hands over the soft fibers and inhaled the clean scent. Alice felt safe here with them. Out of habit, she had tried to suppress her change into her little space, but Alexa had gently coaxed her out of her shell. Alice stood for Alexa to dry her. Alexa did so carefully, increasingly aware of how soft Alice's skin was. She swallowed, feeling desire flash hotly through her.

"John picked these out just for you," Alexa said as she led Alice back into the master bedroom. This time Alice had a good look around. The colors were muted grays and dark greens, giving the room an ethereal, forest-like feel.

"It's so cute," Alice exclaimed excitedly as she held up the onesie that John had laid out on the bed for her. It had a multitude of colorful cartoon sheep pulling various faces printed all over the black material. Alexa helped her get dressed and gently tied the belt of the robe around her waist, "How's that? Not too tight?"

"No, it's just right, Mommy." Alice was feeling lighter. The warmth from the bubble bath and Alexa's gentleness had soothed her nerves.

"What's your favorite flavor soup, baby girl?" Alexa asked, tucking a stray strand of hair behind Alice's ear.

"Chicken."

"That sounds delicious," Alexa said.

"Let's go see what we can do about making you some soup."

"Okay, Mommy."

Chapter 7

"I thought we could take some time off," Alexa offered the next morning when they were all seated around the kitchen table. Alice was happily eating her Fruit Loops, humming along to a song in her head. She had slept like the dead - better than she had in months. Just the thought that John and Alexa were there had made it possible for Alice to relax and stay in her little space as long as she had wanted. She had feared their disgust, but they had happily accommodated her. Alexa had held her as she fell asleep while she sang to her. Alexa's voice was soothing, deep, and it resonated within her. It hadn't taken long before her heavy lids had dragged themselves shut, and Alice had fallen asleep easily, happily and lightly drifting through the songs.

"When do you want me to take you home, Alie?" Alexa asked. Alice froze, spoon halfway to her mouth, milk dribbling onto the counter. The suddenness of her question had startled Alice. She hadn't thought of going home. Did they not want her?

Alice swallowed and set the spoon back in the bowl, surreptitiously wiping the drops of milk away with the sleeve of a borrowed robe. She cleared her throat, feeling suddenly exposed.

"Can...Can't I stay here? With you?" Alice asked, her voice still small. She dreaded the thought of having to go home and deal with whatever waited for her there.

"Just for a little bit?" Alice added.

"We thought you'd, well, want to go home," John said, his gaze flicking from Alexa to Alice and back again. He was surprised that Alice had wanted to stay.

"Of course, Alice," Alexa said, "You're welcome to stay as long as you need."

"Really?" Alice asked, fiddling with the sleeves of the robe, pulling at the loose threads nervously. She wanted to stay in her little space just a while longer. She liked being there with them.

"You're not upset with me?" Alice asked, forcing her lip to stop quivering.

John smiled wide, reflecting the warmth in his eyes, "No, baby girl. You didn't do anything wrong." Alice blinked away the sting of tears and nodded, returning to her Fruit Loops.

"Your clothes are all washed, Alie," Alexa said.

"My clothes?" She blinked in confusion, temporarily forgetting that the robe and onesie were not hers. She glanced at where Alexa had pointed, and a fresh wave of sadness and anger washed over her.

Alice shook her head vigorously, closing her eyes and pursing her lips together. She remembered the boxes that were still waiting for her. Alice's emotions were hot and wild and so very close to the surface the past couple of days that she barely felt the tears roll down her cheeks again.

"Why the tears, sweetheart?" John asked.

"I don't want to wear that." Alice was pointing at her cleaned and freshly pressed work outfit. John looked at Alexa, then back at Alice.

"You don't have to wear it," he said, smiling gently and patting her hand.

"I don't?"

"No," John said, shaking his head.

"But I can't go out like this," Alice said, still sniffling, looking down at herself. Her heart was breaking. She didn't want to dress like a grownup. She didn't want to wear that stupid blouse. It was too plain, and the skirt was itchy. Alice's breath hitched, and she let out a sob. John wiped her cheeks with both his palms and pulled Alice in for a firm hug.

"I've got something that you can wear, Alie," Alexa said. "Then, when we go out, you can buy yourself something you like." John released her, and Alice looked at Alexa, her lashes wet, and her face already puffy.

"I don't have to wear that?" Alice asked again, pointing at the outfit. Alexa shook her head.

"Come now. No more tears, okay?" John said, wiping at the moist trails on her face. Alice nodded and rubbed her chin on her shoulder. She felt squirmy and uncomfortable. She was embarrassed at the way she had reacted. Alexa and John had been gracious, letting her wind down and stay over. They had fed her and cared for her, and she had acted like Alice stopped her thought.

"Let's go get ready, Alie," Alexa said, calling her over, holding her hand out for her. Alice hopped off the stool and shuffled over to her, still fiddling with the cuffs of the robe. Her face was warm, and her tears were very close to the surface again.

She peeked up at Alexa and saw no trace of annoyance on her face. Her smile was genuine, and her eyes were welcoming. Alexa led her back to the room she had spent the night in. It had been decorated to accommodate a little, Alice realized. There were plenty of stuffies and other toys decorating the top of the dresser.

"Do you have your own little?" Alice asked, her eyes taking in the room where she had slept in the daylight. Alexa glanced at her. Her hands paused within the depths of the drawer.

"We've had a few, but after a while, we realized that we were better sharing our love with as many little ones who needed it."

"I had no idea," Alice mumbled, sitting on the bed, examining one of the bear stuffies. It had a little blue bow tie and checkered vest. She smiled and set it back on its spot next to the otter.

"If you want, we can take you to a play party some time," Alexa offered.

"Why?"

Alexa scrunched up her nose and pretended to be very interested in the different pull-ups as she gathered her thoughts.

"You might enjoy spending some time with other littles, or you could even find a Caretaker of your own."

"Oh," Alice said, a little hurt by the implication.

"Oh, here we go," Alexa said and pulled out a lovely muted yellow dress.

"What do you think?"

Alice fell in love with the dress the second she

saw it. It had short, puffy sleeves and soft, ribboned frills that accented the neck and hemlines.

"It's beautiful," she crowed. Alexa smiled and held it up to Alice's form.

"I think you'll make all the other little girls jealous, Alie."

Alice giggled and held the dress to her, twirling around as she watched the fabric and frills ripple with the movement.

"Do you want to come to choose a pull-up? I bought a couple of new ones just last week," Alexa said.

Alice, still holding on to the dress, ran to Alexa and peered into the drawer. There, next to the onesies, were fresh stacks of pull-ups. Alexa unpacked them for her, and Alice landed on one that matched her dress.

"This one with the little owls," Alice said.

"Okay, this one it is. Do you want me to help you get dressed today?" Alexa asked as she shut the drawer and stood.

Alice thought for a moment and nodded. The

buttons on the back of her dress would require an extra pair of hands to close.

"Alright, baby girl."

***

Alice held Alexa's hand the whole time, even though she had been too excited to stand still for very long. Alexa had allowed herself to be led around by little Alice as she flitted from storefront to storefront.

"Oh, look at this!" Alice crowed and dragged her inside. John patiently followed behind, holding their purchases, laughing at the strange looks their little band was eliciting.

"Alright, last stop," John said when he finally caught up with his girls, "I need food." Alice pouted, "But, Daddy, we're having so much fun."

"Alice," Alexa warned. Alice dropped her head a little and mumbled an apology.

"Don't worry, baby girl. We've got plenty of time the rest of the week to go anywhere we want," John said.

"Can we come back tomorrow?" Alice asked, negotiating. She looked longingly at the furry pink jacket that had caught her eye. Alice made a small mental note that even if Mommy didn't want to get it for her, she'd come back on her own.

"What do you think, love?" John asked, wrapping an arm around his wife's waist, pulling her in for a kiss.

"I suppose we could come back after lunch." Alice's eyes lit up.

"But," Alexa added, "Only if you promise to be a good girl. Only good girls get presents." Alice nodded eagerly, her heart soaring, "I promise I'll be good."

"Good girl," John said and kissed the top of her head, wrapping his free arm around her waist, pulling her tightly to him. He didn't care about the looks he was receiving from patrons. He felt that what anyone did in their free time had zip to do with anyone else.

"What do you want to eat?" John asked as

they headed to the food court. As promised, Alice had proven to be an exemplary good little girl. She did still try pushing for a second ice cream cone, but she didn't act out more than that. Alice had held their hands and kept up polite conversation as Alexa and John did some shopping of their own. John had his eye on a brand new Ibanez guitar and played a few bars of the song he was working on to test it. Alice saw the way his eyes lit up, and his entire demeanor changed as soon as he began to play. She glanced at Alexa and saw the deep love she held for him displayed for the world to see.

After some internal debate, John set the guitar back on its stand and spoke to the manager. They exchanged numbers, and John greeted him with a hug and a slap on the back.

"Awesome. Let me know when it comes in."

"What was that?" Alexa asked.

"I may or may not have asked him to let me know the moment a very special girl comes in," John said. Alexa laughed, teasing him.

"A special girl? So you're getting yourself a brand new baby? What about us?"

Alice watched their exchange in silence, a smile on her lips. They made jokes and poked fun once in a while, but never stepped over boundaries. Alice was a little envious of how at ease they were with each other and how safe they felt together. John shrugged, his face turning a slight shade of pink. She playfully pushed his shoulder.

"Is it the cherry red bass?" His face broke into an unbelievably big grin, "You know me so well."

"Did they find you one?" Alexa gasped, her eyes growing wide as she finally understood his excitement. John was giddy, excitement making his eyes tear up, and he nodded. His voice was thick with emotion, "Fender, 1951. A cherry-red, four-string precision bass."

"That's amazing! After how many years, my love?" Alexa hugged him tightly, his excitement bubbling through her, infecting her.

"Is that a good guitar, Daddy?" Alice asked, wanting to be part of the excitement and conversation.

"My granddaddy used to own one just like it before it got destroyed in a fire."

"Oh, no," Alice clapped her hand over her mouth in shock.

"He taught me how to play, and it's because of him that I make music," John said, love in every crease on his face.

"If you want, I can teach you, too, Alie."

***

"I've been to almost all of your concerts, Daddy," Alice said as she licked melted ice cream from her hand. It was unseasonably warm today, but under the cool shade of the oak trees, it was a pleasant day.

"Oh, that is so cool!" John exclaimed, "Which song is your favorite?" He leaned forward excitedly. Music was his passion and finding someone who enjoyed his music always sent a jolt of happiness through him.

"Double Down."

"Double Down? What about Boo You?"
Alexa hid a smile as she watched the two of them
interact. She loved John to the ends of the earth,
and Alice was already growing on her. The girl
was curious, funny, and seemed to fit in rather
well. Alice had taken some time to adjust to
them, but Alexa could tell that she was going to
be a tough nut to crack.

"What about..." John paused for effect,
tapping his finger on his chin, "One More Time?"

"Oh, yes! That one is my favorite!" Alice
said, rocking back, holding onto her knees.

"Really? That's my favorite, too." John
said. Alice giggled, throwing her head back. She
was becoming more comfortable with them, and
it made Alexa happy. The girl needed someone to
take care of her, and she felt that the two of them
were exactly what Alice needed.

"You can't have any favorites!" Alice
exclaimed.

"Why not?" John gasped in mocked
disbelief.

"Because you wrote all those songs,

Daddy. You have to like them all, or you wouldn't play them." John paused for another moment, pretending to think over her words.

"I don't know..." he muttered, "Some of those songs are kinda stupid."

Alice laughed again, her grin lighting up her eyes and face, highlighting her beautiful soul. When she dropped her guard, Alexa could easily see herself falling in love with her. By the look on John's face, she could tell that he was smitten. Alexa hid a smile behind her plastic cup as she drank the fruit juice. There were few families around them, many preferring to spend the day either indoors or at the waterpark for the heat. They had changed their minds, opting for the park instead. Alexa didn't want to deal with large, unruly crowds today. Spending one on one time with Alice was so much more fulfilling than having her distracted by all the different rides. It was peaceful here in the shade of the large tree. Alexa knew that she wanted Alice as her little. Alice seemed to love John, but she knew it could be some time before the girl was completely comfortable with them. It would be some time before she would trust them, but Alexa knew she was willing to put in the effort to win Alice's trust.

"What are you thinking?" John leaned over and whispered in her ear while Alice was distracted by a bee that had flown closer to their treats.

Alexa grinned and kissed him, his warm lips, making her tingle. She pulled away.

"I'm thinking about how much I love seeing the two of you together."

"She's got a good heart," John said.

Their talk was interrupted when Alice let out a small, panicked squeak. The bee had flown too close to her face, and Alice had instinctively swatted at it. This had upset the bee and made it buzz angrily around her.

"Kill it! Kill it!" Alice shrieked and tried to scoot away from it as fast as possible while flailing her hands over her head, trying to protect her face.

"Hold still, Alie," Alexa said in a firm

voice, and she got to her knees to help. She gently ushered the bee away while John made Alice lie down on the blanket and covered her head with her hands. Alexa managed to shoo the bee away and put out a small piece of fruit further away from them in hopes of drawing it that way.

"We don't hurt them, Alie," Alexa said. "It only wanted a little bit of food."

"But it tried to hurt me," Alice whined.

"Only because you tried to hurt it first," John said and helped her sit upright, checking to see if she had any stings.

"Are you hurt?" He asked, trying to draw her attention back to him. Alice was distracted, looking around her for any more bees. When he was satisfied that she was completely unharmed, he kissed the knuckles on both hands and crouched in front of where she sat.

"Come see," John said and held his hand out to her.

"Where are we going?" Alice asked.

"I want to show you that the bees' only

attack if they feel threatened." Together they walked to a nearby flower bush and squatted down. Alice was uncomfortable. She didn't like bees.

"But, Daddy!"

"Just watch," John said and poured a little bit of liquid into the lid of his water bottle and held it out to the bees buzzing around the bush. He felt Alice's grip on his arm tighten.

"It's okay, Alie. Just watch."

So she did. At first, nothing happened. Then a couple of bees buzzed around the lid and carefully landed. She watched as their funny little bee tongues touched the water for a few seconds before taking off again. They ignored the two of them, focusing on the water, zipping back and forth between the flowers and their small gift of water.

"I know they can seem scary, but they're just trying to have a good life," John said. He stroked her hair. Alice giggled, enjoying the attention of John and watched the bees wiggle their yellow butts as they landed.

"They do look kinda cute with their small, fat bodies," Alice said.

"Yeah, they kinda do," John smiled.

***

They slept in late a few days, lazing around the house until mid-afternoon before deciding how they were going to spend their time. Alice had been eager to share her ideas, and while going to the Reptile House for the third time would have made her day, Alexa chose the beach. It was less than a ten-minute walk from their home, and this late in the afternoon, it would be empty. John tickled Alice, and they rolled around on the beach, sand getting in their hair and sticking to their sunscreen-layered skin. It was wonderful to get to know Alice. She was smart and humorous, but her sharp tongue often got her into trouble. They had gone over some rules with her, keeping the list short. Even though Alice hadn't yet shown interest in being with them long-term, it was still important to have rules in place so that they all knew where they stood with one another.

1. No swearing.
2. No running around in public by herself.
3. Help with chores.

Alexa and John felt that, at the very least, having rules in place could help her adjust to the idea of staying with them long-term. Alice hadn't said which way she was leaning as far as becoming a permanent part of their little family, but she did mention next-times and talked in terms of future events. This gave them hope.

John watched the sunset while Alice made crumbly sandcastles next to them. Alice lined her crooked towers with broken seashells and asked Alexa to help take pretty pictures for her Instagram.

Alexa and John would spend each evening in each other's arms, recalling the day and delighting in the pleasure they would have if Alice agreed to be their little.

For the moment, Alice seemed to be content just being herself. She demanded nothing from them and genuinely seemed to enjoy spending time with them.

***

Alice pushed her boundaries with John and Alexa more frequently. She was getting bolder and more confident in herself. When they had asked her to help clean up after dinner, Alice had pouted and refused. While some punishments were put into place, they weren't anywhere near where they could have been. Alexa hadn't wanted to push too hard, and Alice had taken that as a little challenge to see just how much she could get away with.

"Alice, we've talked about this." Alice stomped her foot and stared John down. She didn't want to go to bed. She didn't want to clean. Alice stood firm in her stubbornness. She wasn't tired. She didn't like that she had to be in bed while Mommy and Daddy were awake watching television or doing other things.

"Alice," John said, his voice hard. Alice was pushing their boundaries again, and he wasn't having it this time.

"It's time for bed." Alexa could see the irritation scrunch up his shoulders.

"No."

"Why not?" Alexa asked Alice, placing a calming hand on her husband's arm.

"Because I don't want to."
Alexa gave Alice a stern look.

"Excuse me?"
Alice pouted and lifted her chin in defiance.

"I'm not sleepy. You're still awake, so why can't I be?"

"Growing girls need their sleep, Alie," Alexa said patiently.

"No." Alice knew she was being pig-headed, but she was too far along with her stubborn refusal that she felt it would be dishonest to pull back. Alice glared at them, and they matched her stare for stare.
Alexa sighed.

"You're only going to make your punishment worse if you keep going, Alice."
She shook her head.

"Bedroom. Now," John said. Alice's eyes widened at the anger in his voice. Instinctively, she glanced at his hands and took a step back.

"Alice, go. Please," Alexa said firmly. Alice had gone too far. Finally, she obeyed them and waited in her room for the inevitable.

Alice jumped as the door opened, and Alexa stepped through, a stern, unhappy expression on her face.

"Alie, you know why you were sent to your room, right?" Alexa asked.

Alice nodded.

"Tell me."

"I back talked and didn't do my chores."

"And?"

"I argued."

"Good. Now, let's talk about what you've done." Alexa hated punishing Alice like this, but she had gone too far. Her stubbornness was going to get her into much bigger trouble later on.

"You've been a naughty girl today, Alie," Alexa said.

Alice dropped her gaze to the floor, hanging her head slightly, "But I'm—"

"Alice. Enough." Alexa cut her off and sat on the edge of the bed.

"I'm sorry, Mommy," Alice said, her voice weak and her legs trembling.

"The rules are there for your health and safety, Alice. We don't say the things we do just because we can and want to."

Alice nodded.

"I know."

"Promise me that you'll try to be a better little girl from now on, okay, baby?"

Alice nodded again.

"Use your words, Alie."

"Yes, Mommy. I promise I'll try harder to be a good little girl."

***

"Alice," John said, calling her over to where he and Alexa were setting the table for dinner. She had taken a break from her little space and was getting ready to face the mountain of stuff she had stuffed into a dark corner of her mind.

"Yeah?" By the end of the week, Alice had been able to relax and process the difficult past few days and had managed to set a plan in motion. Alice would spend some time apart from them while she returned home to deal with her adult responsibilities.

"We want you to be our little."
Alice paused and stared at the two of them over the rim of her coffee cup. Her eyes drifted downwards to the paperwork in his hands.

"I know things have been a little difficult for you, but we love spending time with you, and we want you to be ours."
Alice's heart thumped hard.

"Really?"

"Really," Alexa said. Her heart was clamoring in her chest and attempting a steep climb out of her throat. Alice was the perfect fit for the two of them. She fit in with them so completely that it was difficult to see themselves taking another little, or even worse, seeing her with a different Caregiver.

Of course, if that is what she wanted, Alexa would help Alice find a Caregiver who would make her happy and love and treat her with as much kindness and consistency as she needed.

Alexa gripped John's hand so tightly that she could have sworn that she could hear the bones rub against one another, but he did not indicate that it was uncomfortable or painful.

"We will need to review our rules and limits," Alexa added in an attempt to set Alice at ease, "but, yes. We want you to be ours if you'll have us."

"We understand if you don't—"

"Yes."

"What?"

"I said, yes. Yes, I want to be yours."

***

Alice had made herself comfortable on John's lap. She had just woken from a nap, and her hair was wild and unkempt.

"Hi, sleepy-head."

"Hi, Daddy," Alice mumbled and snuggled into his arms. She was warm and comfortable, and felt safe.

"Where's Mommy?" Alice asked.

"She went to shower before dinner." John stroked her hair and gave her a tight squeeze, "Are you hungry?"

Alice nodded.

"Good."

"What are we having?"

"I have no idea. What are you in the mood for?" Alice thought for a moment. "Can we have mac and cheese?"

"Sure," John said.

"But you'll have to help. I don't know how to make it." Alice laughed.

"I'll show you, Daddy."

"Okay, okay."

Alice pressed herself against him. After her punishment last night and sneaking a peek at John and Alexa's alone time, Alice was so worked up that the slightest brush against her body was sending sparks coursing through her.

Alice innocently brushed against John's crotch, and another hot spark shot through her, making her instantly wet. He wasn't fully hard, but she could feel the outline of his thick cock through the jeans. Alice licked her lips and straddled John's lap.

Alexa raised an eyebrow as she walked in, towel drying her hair. Alexa was naked under her robe and felt her body tingle at the sight of their little girl straddling her Daddy.

"What are you doing, baby girl?" John asked an amused smile on his face. She wasn't quite as subtle as she thought she was. Alice would have to use her words if she wanted something.

"Nothing," Alice chimed. She slowly, carefully lowered herself onto his lap, feeling his cock through the layers of material.

Alice met Alexa's gaze, and her Mommy nodded.

"Nothing?" John repeated. "Really?"

Alice's cheeks flushed, and she averted her gaze.

Alexa was watching them.

"Tell me what you want, Alie. Use your words."

Alice leaned down and whispered into his ear, sensually pressing herself against him, "I want you to play with me, Daddy."

John arched a brow and stifled a smile.

"How do you want me to play with you, baby girl?"

"The way you and Mommy played with each other last night."

"Last night?"

"Yes, Daddy."

John brushed her hair out of her face. The thought of Alice watching him fucking Alexa immediately made him hard, and by the knowing look on her face, she could feel his response.

"So, can we, Daddy?" Alice rolled her hips against him.

"You sure about this, baby girl?" John said.

"You haven't asked for this before."

"Yes, Daddy." When John hesitated, Alice

scooted off his lap and reached between her legs. The clasps on her onesie snapped open. She pulled it up over her head and stood in nothing but her thigh high bunny socks.

John drew in a breath through his teeth.

"Good job, Alie," Alexa said and sat next to him on the couch. John glanced at her.

"Sit on Daddy's lap, baby girl."

Alice obeyed. John's gaze slid over her body, her nipples hardening under his gaze, and her pussy moistening as the rough material of the jeans stroked her clit.

"Rub yourself against him," Alexa said.

Alice slowly and rhythmically began rubbing herself against him. Alexa watched, already turned on by this display. Alexa wanted to let Alice do what she wanted, only offering small nudges whenever she noticed her tell-tale moment of uncertainty play across her features. Alice reached between them, unbuttoning his jeans. She slid off his lap and knelt in front of him. His eyebrows shot up.

"Alie, are you sure you want to do this?

You know you don't have to do anything you don't want to, right?"

"I know, Daddy. I want to," She reassured him, her small, warm hands wrapped around his cock as she gently coaxed it free from the confines of his boxers and jeans.

Alice licked her lips and took the swollen head of his shaft into her mouth, maintaining eye contact with him as she ever so slowly lowered her head, taking the length of him into her mouth, opening her throat to let him be enveloped. Alice had watched how Alexa had teased and pleased John, and she copied her.

"Good girl," Alexa said, pleased. She bit her lip when she caught sight of Alice's smooth mound, moisture already coating the folds of her pussy lips in a fine sheen.

Alice took her time pleasing her Daddy, listening to his moans and instructions as she sucked on his cock.

"Stop."

Alice pulled back in time, and he panted as he forced his orgasm from peaking. Alice chewed on her bottom lip and then straddled him on the couch, rubbing the head of his cock against her moist pussy lips.

"Fuck me, Daddy," she said.

Chapter 8

"We've come up with some rules that we think you should follow, Alice," Alexa said as they finalized the last bit of the paperwork.

Alice pulled the sheet of paper closer and read each one out loud.

"Trust and respect, Mommy and Daddy." Alice looked up at John and Alexa and nodded. It made sense, but she also understood why it had to be in her list of rules.

"Always be on your best behavior, and do your chores." Alice frowned at the thought. She hated doing chores. It was why her small apartment looked like a tornado had gone through it more often than not.

"Eat three meals a day." Alice disagreed and told them so.

"I don't eat that much."

"You've got to stay healthy, Alice. I've seen the way you eat," Alexa said.

"But—"

"That brings us to the next one: no backtalk. We've only got your best interests at heart, so we expect you to listen. Eating three meals a day is not unreasonable. If it's still too much, we can adjust the amount of food."

"Bathe daily." Alice liked to bathe, so that wasn't a rule.

"Don't stay up past your bedtime." Again Alice paused and looked at them. "When is my bedtime?"

"9 PM."

"What?"

"Yes. You have to be well-rested for your job during the week."

"What about weekends? Can I stay up later?"

"We can discuss that." John nodded.

"Don't wander off while we're in public." Alice continued reading from the list, her eyes breezing over all of the notes and changes they had made of the rules and regulations. Alice stopped once in a while to offer an opinion on a certain rule if she felt it was unreasonable. Half the time, Alice got her way. The other half, John and Alexa, had put their foot down when she pushed her luck too far, and she was sent to her room as punishment. If Alice continued, they withheld her orgasms.

They agreed on a safe word, just in case.

"And no going into the naughty store without us."

***

John saw the fear in Alice's eyes and immediately pulled back.

"Hey, baby girl, it's okay." He unlocked the cuffs around her wrists and tossed them aside, rubbing her arms. She had chills.

"Alie, you have to tell Daddy when I'm doing something that scares or hurts you," he said and pulled her onto his lap. He could feel her shaking, and it terrified him.

"Daddy," Alice said after she had calmed down enough to stop her hiccoughs, "I don't like being cuffed."

"We're so sorry, baby," Alexa said and gently stroked her hair. It had come as a surprise to all of them.

Alice had been open to the idea, given that it wouldn't hurt, and it was something she could potentially enjoy. It had been meant to be used as an alternative form of punishment, to be unable to touch either Mommy or Daddy during their sexy playtime. Alice had felt too vulnerable - too scared.

She was starting to develop feelings for her Caregivers, and that made her act out more frequently. Because of this feeling of vulnerability, Alice tested her limits. John and Alexa never lost their cool with her. Alice found this a little annoying, and so she continued to push. When she had gone too far, Alexa sent Alice to bed early.

After an agonizing night of staring at the ceiling, Alice walked into their room in the small hours of the morning and went to their room, sneaking in as quietly as she could.

"Mommy?"

"What's wrong, Alie?" Alexa asked, instantly alert.

"Can I sleep here?" Alice asked, her voice small. She needed some physical contact and didn't know how to ask for it, especially since she was afraid that they would send her away because she had been disobedient.

"Of course, Alie," Alexa said, scooting up to make space for her. She snuggled close to Alexa and whispered, "I'm sorry." Alexa's warm arms wrapped around her, and Alice realized with a start that she was wearing a very thin nightshirt and nothing else. Alice's heart pounded in her ears, and her body broke out in goosebumps. She pressed herself closer to Alexa, inhaling her scent. Alexa felt the girl's body pressed against her, the heat of her skin seeping through the thin fabric of her sleepwear.
In the light filtering through the open curtains, Alexa could see her trusting eyes looking up at her.

"Is it okay if I touch you?" Alice

whispered, acutely aware of how her body tingled at every stroke Alexa ran down her back. Alice let her hands trail down Alexa's body and over her shirt. Her fingers skimmed the hem of her sleepwear and touched the soft flesh of Alexa's thighs.

Alexa's breathing had changed slightly, Alice noted, a thrill of success running through her.

"It's okay, baby girl. You can keep going," Alexa said breathlessly as Alice's fingertips stroked her inner thighs.

Alexa massaged Alice's breasts through her onesie, the fabric unable to hide her hardened nipples.

"I want you to touch me, Alie," Alexa whispered to her little girl.

Alice complied, running her hand up Alexa's leg, pushing beneath the hem of her nightshirt. Her fingers found Alexa's curls, stroking through them, feeling her body heat.

"That's a good girl," Alexa muttered, and she toyed with her nipple, gently tugging on it. A soft moan escaped her lips, and Alice's demeanor changed instantly. Her forwardness had evaporated and was replaced by her submissive demeanor.

"Keep going, little girl," Alexa said as she slowly spread her legs, allowing Alice access to her core.

"Yes, Mommy," Alice said, her face burning and her own body throbbing in response to her fingers sliding into Alexa's moist pussy. Alexa inhaled sharply, biting her lip, pleased by Alice's touch. The girl was a quick study. Alice's fingers massaged her, drawing sighs of pleasure from Alexa.

Alice felt the bed shift behind her.

"You need a hand?" John asked, his voice deep and thick with lust and sleep.

Alice met Alexa's gaze and nodded. She desperately wanted him. Her body burned. A glint in Alexa's eyes spread to a smirk.

"Looks like our little girl can't wait for you to touch her."

"But she's been such a bad girl lately," John said, pressing himself against Alice's ass.

His cock was heavy, having listened to Alexa's moans as Alice touched and pleased her Mommy.

Alice whimpered, "I'll be good, I promise." Her fingers stroked deep into Alexa's pussy, and she moaned loudly and arched her back.

"Promise?" John asked as he ran his hands over Alice's ass, stroking the soft flesh. He reached around, unclipping the clasps of her onesie, purposefully stroking her through the fabric.

"Yes," Alice breathed.

"Yes, who?"

"Yes, Daddy." John continued stroking her cleanly shaven lips, coating his fingers in her moisture.

"Little Alie is already so wet, Mommy," John remarked.

Alice's whole body trembled as she let Alexa and John tease and touch her. The two made turns to stroke her, kiss her, and nibble her exposed skin.

"Please," Alice muttered.

"Please, what, Alie?" John growled in her

ear as he rubbed his cock against her opening.

"Please can I cum?"

Alexa gently bit down on Alice's nipple, running her tongue around the hard nub. The girl moaned and bucked her hips, trying to get the release she desperately craved.

"I think we have punished her enough, don't you?" John asked, reaching over to stroke his wife's pussy lips. She was dripping wet from their play and Alice's fingers, and his cock jerked painfully.

"Please...please."

Her moans were causing cum to leak from the head of his cock as he continued to stroke Alexa.

"Bend over for Daddy," Alexa commanded. Alice obeyed, her mind spinning, and her body thrumming. She got onto her knees and spread her legs for him, stretching her hands out to Alexa. Alexa lay in front of Alice, spreading herself open to her gaze. Without being asked, Alice wrapped her hands around Alexa's hips and pulled her closer. As soon as her tongue touched the soft folds of her lips, she felt

John's hard cock press against her twitching pussy, and a desperate whimper escaped her throat. Alexa chuckled, "Stop teasing our little girl, John. I think she's learned her lesson. Isn't that right, Alie?"

"Yes, Mommy. I promise I'll be a good girl." Alice said, her eyes were glassy from desire and unspent lust. Alexa pulled her closer and kissed her, their tongues dancing as she spread Alice's legs apart, allowing better access for John.

A low, guttural growl started in his throat at the sight of them. Alexa was sensually rubbing their bodies together, their broken, hitched breathing causing his mind to reel. John closed the gap and gripped Alice's hips, interlacing his fingers with his wife's as she held on. He thrust his hardness into Alice's hot, wet pussy. Her body reacted instantly, clamping down on his cock, twitching and pulsing as he pushed deeper inside of her. Alice moaned loudly. All thoughts of behaving fled from her mind. She bucked against him and locked her fingers in Alexa's hair, the other hand finding her core. Alice inserted two fingers into Alexa's pussy, not as gently as she had earlier.

"Fuck," Alexa moaned.

John stroked his cock in and out of Alice's pussy, enjoying the feel of the warmth of her body around him. His breathing was already ragged. The sight of his two beautiful girls giving each other pleasure had pushed him dangerously close to the edge.

Alice moaned into Alexa's mouth and felt her orgasm threaten. She gasped, biting down on Alexa's shoulder, her nails leaving light scratches down her side. She had slipped her fingers out of Alexa's pussy, bracing herself on either side of her body as John thrust wildly into her. Stars burst in front of her vision as soon as Alexa touched her clit with her fingertips. Her scream caught in her throat, her pussy clamped and pulsated around John's thick cock, and Alexa breathed into her ear, sending waves of pleasure and chills rippling over and through her body.

Alice had been edging her orgasm for days, and the sudden release made her vision blur, and her whole body convulse and twitch. Her body shook as John fucked her, panting as he came, shooting his cum into her tight pussy.

John continued to thrust into Alice, feeling his cum and her juices leak from her hole, spreading down her thighs to stain the sheets. Her body clamped around him, and he felt a second orgasm build.

"Let me lick you, Mommy," Alice whispered into Alexa's ear. She moved back, exposing herself to Alice's waiting tongue, oblivious to the rising sun lightening the room.

Chapter 9

Alice looked at them, her jaw working and her breathing speeding up. She was utterly overwhelmed by their kindness. It conflicted deeply inside her with what she knew about everyone she had ever come into contact with. David had been oppressive and egotistical about their relationship - demanding and one-sided. Alice had lacked love and kindness from the very people who were sworn to protect and care for her.

Alexa and John shared a look.

"Alice, sweetheart, you need to talk to us." They didn't argue or scream. They only punished her when she was bad and never withheld care. They guided her with love and kindness, and it scared her. They took care of her, and they looked out for her.

Alice wanted so badly to be theirs. She wanted them to love her as much as they loved each other. She wanted to be part of their family. That feeling deep inside her made her uneasy. Still, she couldn't suppress the feeling that they were going to discard her the way her parents had. She couldn't bear losing her Mommy and Daddy. Alice's heart stalled in her chest when she realized that she was beginning to grow attached to them - that she had fallen in love with them.

"I'm going out."

"Alice—"

"I want to go to the mall, and I want to go alone."

Alice had been snarky all afternoon, being as bratty as possible, fighting against any rule they had tried to reinforce, and she all but screamed at them to leave her alone.

Alice had nearly burst into tears when John took her aside and just hugged her. She had pushed him away, rejecting his touch, but he didn't object. He only smiled at her and said, "It'll be okay kiddo." No lecture, no fights - just a hug.

He called her for dinner later that night, and Alexa had drawn a bath for her before bedtime.

They didn't treat her any differently. Alexa asked her about her day and allowed her to watch whatever she had wanted.

When it came time for bed, Alexa had gotten her room ready and even had Beanie waiting for her under the covers, tucked in as if he was asleep.

Alice didn't acknowledge or thank them. She glared at Beanie. She glared at Alexa when she said goodnight.

Alice fell into a restless sleep, her nightmares turning their kindness into manipulation and abuse.

The next morning, Alice approached Alexa before breakfast. She had hoped to speak to her before John woke up, but when she got there, he was already brewing a fresh pot of coffee for them.

"Alexa," Alice said quietly. "I…"

Alexa gave her a moment to think, but when it became clear that she wasn't going to say anymore, she spoke, "You know you are free to go whenever you want, Alice."

The words struck Alice with force she didn't

expect. It was what she wanted, but why did Alexa's words hurt so much.

Alice clenched her fists.

"I'll leave then."

"That's not what we're saying, Alice," John said, trying not to make her any more uncomfortable than she already was.

Alice looked at him.

"You're not kicking me out?"

"Of course not, Alie," Alexa said, smiling gently.

"We love having you here."

"Then why did you say that?"

"We want you to know that you're not stuck here. We would never dream of forcing you to do anything you didn't want to do," Alexa said.

Alice's lip quivered. Her emotions were confusing to her. She was scared of how happy she had been over the last week, and it wasn't just the sex.

They were taking care of her, making her lunch, and cooking her favorite meals. And they were letting her be in her little space as long as she wanted. They gently reminded her of the rules and afforded the appropriate punishment, but they never overstepped the boundaries she had put in place. She stomped her foot and walked away, slamming her bedroom door behind her. Alice threw herself onto the floor, kicking her legs in the air, screaming into her pillow. She was shaking, her head hurt, and she desperately wanted them to fight back.

She wanted a reason to leave, but they were kind and understanding. Alice's mind drifted to her parents. She had been forced to leave or get drawn into their shitty lifestyle.

She had been alone even before she had left. Alice didn't know how to behave, especially not when John and Alexa were perfect. Again, Alice avoided them and spent a night thrashing and wishing for dawn.

When dawn finally broke, Alice was staring at the ceiling of her bedroom. Alice sighed. She was torn, the tension causing her stomach to cramp and her muscles to ache from keeping them bunched up.

She chose to have a shower. It was time to make a grown-up decision, and she had run from her troubles long enough.

Alice poured herself coffee from the pot as soon as it was done brewing. This was part of Alexa's routine, Alice had learned. It was nice not to have to struggle with the machine so early in the morning. There was a cold nip in the air when Alice stepped outside, closing their front door behind her.

She was going to take an Uber back to her place. She ignored the frantic texts from Alexa and John until the Uber stopped outside her apartment block.

I'm safe. She texted her reply and set her phone to silent.

She would need to sort her thoughts out before she returned to them.

***

"I don't want to move in," Alice said

finally.

"Okay," Alexa said, waiting for Alice to continue.

"I—" Alice's throat closed up, and she tried to clear it unsuccessfully, "I like having my place."

"I like knowing that I'm not dependent on anyone," Alice added.

"Alie, honey? It's okay to need people and it's okay to want your own space. It doesn't have to always one extreme or the next," Alexa explained.

Alice shook her head. She agreed, but she was trying to keep from freaking out again. She cleared her throat again.

"I don't want to move in."

"We know, honey," John replied.

"You don't have to," Alexa said.

"But I still want to visit. I still want you to be my Mommy and Daddy," Alice quickly added.

"Would you like to set up a schedule?" John suggested. Alice nodded. She needed her place. It was hers. She had busted her ass to afford it and then busted her ass to clean it and make it liveable. She felt safe there.

"I'm going to go for a walk, and when I come back, we can talk," Alice said.

John and Alexa let her go, affording her the space she had asked for.

Alice had walked up and down the beach until the sun had set, and a cool wind tugged at her sweater. Alice had finally made up her mind and trudged through the sand back to the house.

"Alexa? John?" Alice asked, drawing their attention away from the television. She closed the distance between them and sat down at the end of the single-seater, facing them. They looked at her, taking in the atmosphere, and they sat up in their seats.

"I need to explain some things."

Alice saw the trepidation on Alexa's face and had to stop herself from aborting her plan and just letting it be.

"Go ahead," John said.

"I grew up in a weird place," Alice said haltingly. She had never told anyone about her past, at least not the way she was planning on telling them now. This was a bare-all, no-holds-barred kind of conversation and one she had been dreading, but here they were.

"I'm going to tell you everything, and I know it could get weird and dark, but I need you to understand certain things about me, and if you think it's something you can't deal with, then I understand." Alice rushed, trying to utter the words before she chickened out.

"But it's something I need to share, or..." Alice stopped short, already feeling the tears threaten to fall. "I feel that you need to know."

"Go ahead, Alice. We promise to listen before making a decision," John said, holding his wife's hand tightly. Alice clasped her hands together and shoved and pinned them between her knees.

"Okay."

She swallowed and started talking, barely hearing her own words over the rushing blood in her ears. She explained everything - what life was like with her parents, the day she left, the messes she got into, and how it had taken so much time and energy to drag her ass back out.

"I don't get close to people," Alice said. "They are unpredictable, and I don't know how to deal with being happy. Happy. For the first time since I was three, maybe." Alice saw a glitter of something in Alexa's eyes before she turned her head away.

"So the attitude, the fights, everything—" John was interrupted.

"The bratty attitude, the..." Alice paused, staring at the ceiling.

"I was scared, and I don't know how to deal with this." Alice waved her hands around, indicating she was speaking of everything, and she looked back at the two of them.

"I don't know how to accept that someone is willing to take care of me."

"I'm sorry that you had to go through that," John said.

"I'm not okay with it," Alice said, "Not yet, but I will be."

"What about other family?" John asked,

aware of his wife's shaking. She had a soft heart, and loving this girl was making the risk of losing her nearly too great to accept.

"They disowned us. My mom stole from everyone and..." Alice looked at the way Alexa was turned away and thought that this was it. This was the moment Alexa would ask her to leave. She was broken, and Alice was giving them every reason to ask her to leave.

"I'm telling you, so you know everything. I'm not good, and you deserve a little that can make you happy," Alice said.
Alexa stood and walked to the kitchen.

"I didn't..." Alice's eyes were wide. She was tense, waiting for the shoe to drop.

"It's okay," Alexa said, smiling. The glittering Alice had seen tears. She had gone to fetch a paper towel to wipe away the smeared mascara.

"It is?" Her voice was shaking now.

"We still want you, Alice," Alexa said. "Your past doesn't define you."

"Yeah, but it's still playing a lead role in

the mess in my head," Alice said. She closed her eyes and rubbed her hands over her face to psych herself up. She wasn't done.

Alice explained the circumstances of her leaving home and those surrounding her parent's death. When she was finished, Alice cleared her throat and looked at each of them in turn.

"I'm sorry for the way I acted," Alice said. Alexa opened her mouth to reply, but Alice shook her head.

"I mean it. I was a right ass to both of you, and I still can't figure out why you didn't just throw me out."

Alexa smiled warmly, "Alie, we like having you here. We want you to be ours, and everything that comes with it. You're not difficult, but just going through some stuff."

"How could we possibly think of throwing you away, Alice?" John said, putting an arm around her shoulders, squeezing gently. "Just...talk to us, okay?"

Alice looked at him, tears welling up again. She hated that she was so emotional. Alexa and John made her feel safe to be herself, and it completely unsettled her, but the kindness they radiated made her want to stay and be part of their family so much that she felt it like a physical ache in her chest.

"I'm trying," Alice said, returning their smiles.

***

"You can still stay here as long as you need," Alexa offered. Alice had noticed that she was acting differently. Less warm and less like herself. Alice supposed it was to give her the space she had wanted.

"Are you mad at me?" Alice asked, drinking the tea Alexa had made for them. John had a rehearsal session, so it was just the two of them.

Alexa turned to face her, taking a moment to absorb the girl sitting across from her at the breakfast nook.

"I'm not mad at you, Alice. You're your

own person, and if you felt that we were pushing too hard, all you had to do was tell us."

Alice looked down at her cup.

"We want you to be happy here, and if we're not doing that—"

"I am happy."

"What?"

"I said that I am happy," Alice repeated.

"You and John are amazing. I've never felt safer than I do with you two." She paused.

"It's why—"

"I know," Alexa said. "You don't need to explain it again."

"But I do," Alice said, her voice rising an octave or two. She felt bad for treating them the way she had.

"I was such a brat."

"You were hurting and confused is all," Alexa said.

"Please, just listen," Alexa repeated.

"You have no obligation here, Alice. Truly. If you want to go, you can go, but give yourself a chance at finding true happiness."

Alexa smiled and patted her hand, pouring them more tea while they listened to the ocean.

It was a little awkward at first after she had poured her soul out to them. She hadn't known how to act, and Alice felt a little out of place, wandering around the house. John had returned from rehearsals, and after calling for Chinese takeout, he got comfortable with Alexa on the couch. Alice had isolated herself to the playroom, which was technically her bedroom now, Alice thought, and she carefully straightened and neatened everything that wasn't nailed down. She had worried about their reaction, but there had been nothing for her to be worried about. They had been concerned, appalled, and completely horrid, as they should have been, but not once did they pass judgment on her, her choices, or those of her family's. Alice took some time to accept the fact that both John and Alexa had wanted her. She changed into her pajamas and finally left to join them.

John heard her approach.

"Come here, baby girl," John said, patting the couch beside him. Alexa had wrapped her arms around John and buried her face in the crook of his shoulder while they were watching some romantic movie on Netflix.

Alice watched the two of them together and made the second hardest decision of her life. She walked over to them and sat next to them. She watched the movie with them, eventually putting her head on Alexa's lap, her fingers running through her hair, washing away the rest of her unease.

"Thank you," Alice whispered, and eventually, she fell asleep on her lap, happy and content.

Chapter 10

Alice ended up spending a lot more of her free time with Alexa and John. Alexa and John had given her time and space to process, even when she became unmanageable.

After Alice had thrown her spoon across the room and stormed off, she had come back to clean up her mess to find that they had already done it.

"I..." Alice stammered and stopped talking, wringing her hands together. She was still adjusting to expressing herself in non-destructive ways. Alice had to fight her urge to run away whenever she felt tight bands of anxiety encircle her chest.

Alice chewed on her lip for a moment and then typed something on her phone. Alexa was about to place a hand on her to get her attention, but she stopped when John shook his head.

"We've got this," John said, kissing the back of his wife's hand.

She showed what she typed.

Thank you for trying to understand. Followed by, I'm sorry.

"It's okay, baby girl," John said, "It's good that you're talking about things that upset you."

"I'm not used to all these feelings," Alice admitted.

John and Alexa waited. After a while, watching her struggle with getting the right words, Alexa gave her a soft hug.

"Take your time, Alice."

Alice inhaled deeply through her nose and let it out through her mouth in a rush. She started typing on her phone again, pacing up and down, and a little quirk she had picked up from Alexa whenever she was on the phone, stamping out fires.

I like you, and I still want to be your little girl

Alice observed their faces, expecting to see the characteristic masking that her parents had often utilized in front of visitors and other people. The walls never went up, but their reactions still surprised her. John and Alexa both threw their arms around her in a tight group hug, planting kisses on her eyes, cheeks, nose, and anywhere they could reach. Alice giggled and squirmed.

"That tickles!"

"Does that mean you want me, too?" Alice asked.

"Of course!" They said in unison.

"You are so very special, Alie," Alexa said, still hugging her nearly too tightly (though Alice didn't mind). Together they worked on helping Alice express herself, especially when she felt overwhelmed. It happened more often than not where Alexa or John would sit with her in a quiet area in the house and do breathing exercises with her after Alice had shut down on them. They had found a pretty cool app that allowed her to select an emoji or self-uploaded face that corresponded with a mood or feeling, and they worked up from there.

"I'm scared," Alice admitted again later that day.

"What are you scared of?" John asked,

sitting across from her.

"That you and Alexa will get tired of me," Alice said. Her eyes were closed, and she was following John's breath, breathing in and breathing out in time with his rhythm.

"It feels surreal," Alice added.

"I understand."

They breathed in the silence. Alice was finally able to get her fight or flight response under control. The rushing of blood and anger in her ears no longer so loud. She wanted John and Alexa to be proud of her, so she tried her hardest.

"Alice, you should know that if you do want to leave, we'll help you find someone you'd be happy with."

Alice stifled the panic. Her knee-jerk reaction was to withdraw and question the meaning behind his words. It took a long moment before she was able to speak again without letting her emotions strangle her words.

"I don't want anyone else."

John was quiet for a moment, and Alice opened her eyes to look at him. He was watching her, a crooked smile on his face, and his eyes twinkling.

"What?" She asked.

"It makes me very happy to hear that, Alie."

"Really?"

"Really. Please trust that when we say we want you here, we mean it."

Alice's eyes burned, and she closed them, trying to calm her racing heart, but she couldn't stop herself from smiling.

"How do you feel?" John asked when the timer announced their session was over.

"Happy." Alice embraced it, and even though right beneath the happiness she was scared, she was starting to hope.

She had pulled a few of her usual stunts after that, throwing tantrums and acting like a complete brat on occasion, but eventually, Alice had fallen into her new routine. She even offered to make dinner (with supervision, of course).

Alice had been worried that the damage she had done would be irreversible, but those worries had held no water. John and Alexa had carefully nurtured her and, when needed, they had punished her for breaking the rules. Yet they never hurt her or made her feel weird about being herself.

And if things got too tough, Alice could retreat to her room knowing she would be safe. Alexa had suggested that her room was for Daddy and Mommy time only. Even so, there was never any expectation other than being a good girl and following the rules. They respected her space.

***

"I have a new toy I want to try out, Mommy," Alice whispered, her face burning red hot. Curious, John cocked his head and watched as she shifted from one foot to the next, her hands behind her back.

"What is it, Alie?"

Very slowly and very carefully, Alice pulled a black cloth bag from behind her back. Her face burned hotter, and she didn't make eye contact with him. She blushed more and then looked at

Alexa.

"I want to show Mommy first."

Alexa caught her meaning and raised her brows at John.

"Oooh, I'm very intrigued."

"Fine," John said dramatically, throwing his head back on the couch. Alice and Alexa laughed and went into the other room.

Alice closed the door behind her.

"What is it, Alie?"

Alice pressed her ear to the door to make sure that John hadn't decided to eavesdrop on them. She wanted to surprise him.

Alexa had an amused smile on her lips, watching her little girl act so secretively. When Alice was satisfied that John wasn't going to spy on them, she opened the wrapping and showed her.

"I thought you and Daddy might like it," Alice said, her ears burning. She had never been one to play outside of her very limited comfort zone, but she wanted to try something that would both surprise and delight them.

Alexa held the item up for inspection. The fur on

the tail was soft and full, attached to a small silicone butt plug. Alexa admired how well the tail had been attached to the plug.

"It is so pretty, baby girl. Did you pick it out yourself?"

"The lady at the store said that the silicone was better because I hadn't done this before," Alice said, feeling a little awkward.

Alexa arched a brow.

"You went into the naughty store by yourself?"

Alice flushed her heart racing. She had forgotten about that one rule. Whoops. She averted her gaze and nervously chewed on the inside of her cheek. She crossed her arms in front of her and shifted her weight, her body already tingling under Alexa's gaze.

"You broke a rule, baby girl."

"It was supposed to be a surprise." The words rushed out, "I wanted to go find something we could enjoy together."

She held her breath. Alexa considered the situation for a moment and smiled, "Okay, but just this once. If you want to go to the naughty store again, tell Daddy or me." Alice nodded in earnest.

"I promise."

"Good girl."

Alexa instructed Alice to strip down and get on the bed.

"You ready, baby girl?"

"Yes, Mommy."

"Spread your thighs for me," Alexa said, shaking a bottle of lube as she admired the sight of Alice on their bed, naked, spreading herself open with her hands.

"Is this okay?"

"Scoot up just a bit. I don't want you to fall off the edge, Alie."

There was a tense moment of anticipation, and Alice squirmed as the cold gel dripped on her asshole. Alexa's fingers were hot against her skin as she massaged the lubricant around the entrance. The lubricant warmed up quickly. Alexa continued massaging and added more gel as was needed.

"Relax, baby girl," Alexa whispered, applying pressure. Alice inhaled sharply, and instinctively pulled away. Alexa simply continued the process: massage, then a bit of pressure. After a short while, Alice opened up to the sensation, actively pressing back against Alexa's fingers. Alexa inserted her well-lubricated finger into Alice's ass hole, and with her free hand, gently stroked over her pussy lips. Alice shivered. Alexa could feel when Alice relaxed enough for her to continue stroking, carefully applying pressure, and stretching Alice out. When Alice's body began quivering, Alexa added a second, well-lubricated finger. Alice's breathing had become shallow and short.

"Good girl, Alie." Alexa slowly pulled away from Alice and added a generous coating of gel to the silicone plug, careful to miss the fur.

"Remember to try and relax, okay?" Alexa asked, pressing the head of the plug against her ass hole, meeting resistance. Alice whined and bit into the pillow.

"Let me know if I should stop, baby,

okay?" Alexa said.

"Keep going." Alice was panting, forcing herself to relax as Alexa rubbed more lubricant onto her hole. Pressure caused her eyes to water, but a fresh rush of arousal flushed through her system the moment Alexa pushed the head of the plug in. Alice's eyes rolled into the back of her head, and she panted as her body relaxed around the butt plug.

"Good girl, Alie," Alexa whispered and stroked Alice's ass. Her panties were clinging to her pussy lips, damp from her arousal. Alice's soft grunts of pleasure had set her core burning hotter than she had been in days.

"You ready to show Daddy?"
Alice exhaled shakily, her face flushed as she sat up.

"It feels weird."

"Does it hurt?"

"Not anymore." Alice smiled.

"Maybe I can help make it feel less weird." Alexa offered. Alice recognized the glint in her eyes and licked her lips. Alice nodded.

Alexa moved to sit in front of Alice.

Alice was sitting on her knees, legs slightly apart as she adjusted to the fullness in her ass. She had changed into a cute little nightdress while Alexa had washed lubrication from her hands. It was soft to the touch and clung to her curves. The tail of the butt plug peeked out beneath it. Alice had her hands braced beside her, gently moving her body, accepting the intrusion. Alexa reached between Alice's legs, never breaking eye contact with her, lightly stroking the skin on her thighs as she did so.

Alice bit her lip and subtly spread her legs apart, allowing her Mommy access to the parts of her that were begging to be touched. When Alexa's fingers touched the smooth skin of her outer lips, a smile spread over her face.

"You're already wet, baby."

Alice nodded, blushing furiously. Alexa's openness and gentle voice made her feel less self-conscious. Alexa slipped her fingers between the folds, playing with her clit, watching Alice's facial expression change as her Mommy touched her so intimately. Her little girl quivered, opening her legs wider for Alexa as she pushed her fingers into her. Alexa brought her fingers to her lips, licking Alice's juices from them, sucking on them. Alice's breathing hitched, her body hot and heavy, her eyes locked on Alexa.

"Let's go show Daddy your surprise."

"Do you think he'll like it, Mommy?" Alice asked.

"I think he'll love it so much he would ask you to wear it for him every night," Alexa said.

"Do I look okay?"

"You're so beautiful, Alie."

"Should I change my hair?"

Alexa ran her hands through her hair, and an idea struck her. She hurriedly went searching for some small ribbons she had lying around.

"There we go." Alexa smiled.

"Now, your outfit is complete."

Alice shakily got to her feet, holding on to Alexa's offered hand.

Alexa's fingers had masterfully manipulated her body to the edge before she stopped, causing

Alice to be unsteady on her feet. She walked hand-in-hand with Alexa back to where John was waiting as he worked on what Alice and Alexa assumed to be lyrics for a new song.

"Daddy?" Alice said softly.

"You two were gone a pretty long time." He looked up from his notepad, and his jaw dropped. Alexa had carefully tied Alice's hair up into two space buns with bright pink ribbons to match her nightdress. The cotton fabric was light, and John could make out the dark areolas of her nipples, already stiff. His gaze drifted further down, resting at the top of her thighs where the dress ended. The light skin contrasted brightly against the deep color of the fabric. His cock strained against his jeans.

"Turn around so you can show Daddy," Alexa prompted. There was a light to her eyes that John recognized whenever she felt particularly mischievous.

"What are you up to?" His words were barely out when Alice did a little twirl. The gray fur of the tail wrapped gently around her leg and swayed behind her when she came to a stop, facing him.

"Slowly," Alexa said, her eyes locked on her husband.

"Okay," Alice said, feeling more and more comfortable as she moved with the butt plug in. She particularly liked the feel of the soft fur on her thighs.

Alice turned slowly, tiptoeing around, pausing with her back to him. Alice giggled, excitement making her wiggle her butt from side to side. That was precisely what Alexa had been waiting for. Her smirk had turned into a grin, and she held Alice in place.

"What do you think, Daddy?" Alice asked, peering over her shoulder at him.

"Wiggle your tail for Daddy, Alie," Alexa prompted.

Alice obliged, delighting in the sounds of barely-controlled desire coming from behind her. Alice looked at Alexa through her lashes; her bottom lip still caught between her teeth.

"Can I do another twirl?"

"Of course, baby girl," John replied. Alice grinned happily and twirled again, faster this time, giggling as the tail swished around her legs. She twirled around again, the hem of her dress rising with her arms. John clenched his teeth and sat forward in his seat. The way Alice's hair had been tied up made her look perfectly wolf-like. Her eyes were big, glittering with excitement, and her smile was infectious.

John made to reach for Alice, but Alexa stopped him, a grin on her face and a devious glint in her eyes.

"No, no. Not yet."

"Why?" John breathed and pressed the palm of his hand against his groin as he leaned back in an attempt to lessen the discomfort.

"You'll get your turn. It's Mommy's turn now," Alexa said and began unbuttoning her blouse.

John's eyes grew wide.

"You're evil. You know that?" He was grinning but growled through his teeth at her. Alexa was going to tease him within an inch of his life. His cock was already throbbing against the zipper, his jeans becoming more and more uncomfortable as he watched Alice do another small twirl before Alexa went to stand behind her.

"Yes, Daddy, it's Mommy's turn." Alice giggled.

Alice gently tugged on the hem of Alexa's robe, exposing her pussy to his gaze. Even in the dim light, he could make out the moisture that coated them and her thighs. She was already wet and waiting. His cock jerked. Alexa stroked Alice as she kept her eyes on John. He rubbed himself through his jeans.

"No touching," Alexa said.

"Yeah, Daddy, no touching," Alice repeated and giggled. Her humor was cut short as Alexa delved between the folds, searching for her core, her fingers still drawing hot trails over her skin. John balled his fists behind his head, his willpower waning as he watched his wife finger Alice. The girl had her head thrown back, her eyes closed, and her legs were buckling. She was small enough that Alexa had no trouble supporting her weight. She lifted Alice's leg, exposing her core to John's gaze, where her fingers were rhythmically pushing in and out. Alice's breath hitched, and Alexa pulled back.

"Not yet, Alie."

Alice protested and pressed herself against Alexa, her nails digging into Alexa's forearm.

"You don't want me to withhold your pleasure entirely, do you?" Alexa warned. "Bad girls don't get to have release."

Alice shook her head.

"I'm sorry, Mommy."

Alice removed her nightdress as her Mommy had instructed and blushed as she caught John openly staring at her. Her gaze dropped to his lap, where his bulge was obvious, and she licked her lips. Alexa put on a little show for her husband. She could see the muscles in his jaw, working as he fought to control himself. She twirled around, suckled on Alice's nipples, and had her help Alexa undress. She enjoyed the sensation of Alice's short nails scraping over her skin as she undid the buttons on Alexa's blouse. Without being prompted, Alice lowered her head to Alexa's nipple and pulled the stiff little nub into her mouth. The sudden sensation spread chills over her body, making her tingle with anticipation. Alice felt Alexa's hands on the back of her head, gently holding onto her as her tongue flicked over her nipple. With her free hand, she massaged Alexa's other breast, her fingertip tracing the outline of her areola, drawing spirals until she flicked gently over the tip. Alice repeated the motion in the opposite direction as she tugged on Alexa's nipple with her teeth, flicking her tongue back and forth over the sensitive nub. Alexa lay down on the carpet and beckoned Alice over, spreading her legs wide. She dropped to her knees next to her.

"John?" Alexa asked.

"Would you like some help with that?" She licked her lips and looked pointedly at his crotch. The dark look of desire in her gaze made him groan out loud.

"Fuck, yes," John said and stood. His

hands immediately went to his fly and popped the button. The heaviness of his cock pressing against the zipper made it slide down an inch before stopping. Alice's eyes followed the dusting of dark hairs peeing from beneath the shirt down behind the zipper of his jeans.

"Help, Daddy, Alice." Alexa's voice was dripping with lust, her fingers quickly bringing her close to an orgasm as she watched John take a step toward them.

John paused in front of Alice, his cock jerking, making the teeth of the zipper slip apart ever so slightly. Having Alice kneel in front of him like this was driving him insane. The tail seemed to naturally follow the curve of her body and match the movement of every shift. He was mesmerized by little Alice. When her hand reached up and touched the metal tab of the zipper, his cock jerked, and he felt cum bead and trickle slowly over the head. Alice knew from experience just how big John's cock was. She fantasized about having him inside her whenever she was spending the week alone at her place. Yet, she couldn't help her eagerness in freeing him or the excitement she felt when she finally held him in her hands. She wiped at a drop of cum and licked it from the pad of her finger.

"Take Daddy's cock into your mouth, baby girl," Alexa whispered, watching as his cock pulsed in anticipation. Her body twitched as she came closer and closer to finishing herself off. Alice took John as deep as it could go, his girth filling up her small mouth. John grabbed her head and laced his fingers through the hair, taking hold of her, controlling the depth and speed of his thrusts, impatient with how torturously slow Alice was taking things.
She looked up at him from beneath her lashes and resisted, that same mischievous glint in her eye that Alexa had had. Reluctantly, he released her and stood back, panting.

"Baby girl." His voice was pleading, cum drops appearing after each small spasm of his cock.

"Not yet, Daddy," Alice said, complying Alexa's words. Alexa had planned to ride John's cock as she came, but the thought was shattered when Alice scooted closer. She reached over to her, running her hand against the soft inner skin of her thigh. Her fingers trailed up, searching. As Alice's fingers made contact with her mound, she arched her back, all plans of taking it slowly dissolving with each soft stroke. Alice ran her hand over her mound, the short hair tickling her palm. Alice circled her thumb over Alexa's clit. Her Mommy moaned, and Alice smiled, "Am I doing okay?"

"Perfect, baby girl," Alexa said, enjoying the attention of her little girl. Alice ran her tongue over Alexa's clit, tasting her juices. Alice sat up, her fingers returning to Alexa's pussy, pushing two fingers into her moist depths. She leaned over and pulled a nipple into her mouth, rhythmically pumping her fingers into Alexa's pussy, feeling her body twitch around them. Alexa moaned.

"Keep going, baby girl, just like that." Alice fingered her, keeping her pace steady, gently tugging on her nipple with her teeth, suckling on it.

"You're such a good girl. You're doing so well," Alexa said, her head leaned back against the floor and her arms reaching for purchase. Alice's heart rose. She liked being called a good girl. It sent a tingle through her body, and her pussy twitched as she thought about how happy Alexa sounded.

"Keep going, baby girl," Alexa encouraged her. She glanced at John, his cock hanging out of his jeans, thick and heavy. The head glistened, and his cock twitched as he watched them. Alice slowed down slightly, eliciting a sound of frustration from Alexa.

"Alie."

She brought her tongue to Alexa's swollen lips, delving between the folds, finding the delicate button that would push Alexa over the edge.

"Oh, fuck."

Alice sped up her thrusts, curling her fingers slightly, stroking the inner, ribbed walls of Alexa's tight pussy. She shuddered and grunted in response to Alice's tongue and fingers working her closer to her climax. John took his painfully hard cock into his hand and squeezed it lightly a few times. He was attempting to stave off the orgasm he could feel dangerously close to the surface. He wrapped his fingers around his shaft tightly this time, pinching the head of his cock between his thumb and finger.

Alexa cursed as she came.

"On the floor, Daddy," Alice said, giggling, her fingers still working in and out of Alexa's pussy. Dazed and holding on by sheer willpower, John obeyed her, his eyes never leaving her face. Alice licked her lips again, her heart beating furiously, encouraged by John's obvious arousal and by Alexa's soft sighs of pleasure as she came down from her orgasm.

She carefully tugged the waistband of his jeans down over his hips, fully freeing his cock. Alice trailed her fingertips down his legs as she slid his jeans to his knees. She stood over him, straddling him, a grin on her face.

"Can I sit on your lap, Daddy?" Alice asked with feigned innocence, swirling her fingers over her clit, sending sparks of heat through her.

John could only nod and watch as she lowered herself to her knees, slowly impaling herself on his cock. The joy on her face nearly broke him, but he grasped the leg of the coffee table, his knuckles turning white from the force of it. Alice slowly rocked herself against him, forcing his thick shaft deeper into her pussy. Alexa crawled over to them and kissed him deeply as Alice rode him.

Strands of her pink hair had escaped from their buns and were now tickling her neck and back as she threw her head back, savoring the tightness of having both her holes filled.

"Can I make Daddy cum yet?" Alice asked, her body hot and throbbing.

"Not yet," Alexa said with a giggle.

"I think you should get off and come here."

Alice obeyed, his cock springing free as she went to where Alexa had pointed. She had changed places with her, Alexa now straddling John in the same way she had.

"Touch yourself for Daddy," Alexa whispered breathlessly as she lowered herself onto John's cock. She moaned sensually and gyrated her hips, eliciting an answering moan from him. Alice spread herself open to his gaze, her fingers finding her soft folds, running her fingers through her juices.

"Good girl," John muttered. He clasped his hands together behind his head, fighting the urge to touch either of them. Alexa lifted herself away from him, his cock pulling free, pulsing once, and bigger drops of pre-cum dribbling down his shaft.

Alexa took his cock into her mouth, tasting herself on him, mixing with his pre-cum. His cock jerked in her mouth, and his balls tightened. John panted and growled, holding on to his sanity by the skin of his teeth. Alexa knew exactly how to break him, and she enjoyed every minute of it. He watched as Alice inserted first one finger, then another, into her pussy. She was sitting too close to him. All he had to do was reach out, and he would be able to touch her. One soft pull and she would be close enough for his touch to do what he had wanted since she had walked into the room. One soft pull and he could put his lips to her dripping wet pussy, lick her soft folds, and suckle on her swollen clit. Alice saw the lust in his eyes, and a thrill went through her. It was a different dynamic this time. Alexa had wanted to tease John, and Alice could tell that he had loved every torturous moment of it. While she had been a little reluctant at first, seeing the smile on his face and the gaze that could devour her, Alice had grown more comfortable in her role as a seductress. Denying him made him fuck harder, it made him more desperate, and Alexa loved that about him. She wanted Alice to experience that same side to him. She wanted her to experience John's cock when there were no barriers and no caution.

Alice fingered herself, stroking her clit in just the right way to edge her closer to an orgasm. Her whole body trembled, and she breathed hard.

"Don't cum yet, Alie," Alexa said as she

lowered herself onto John's cock again. Hot and thick, he filled her, stretching her pussy walls as she stroked him. She could feel the heat of his thick shaft, warming her from the inside. His cock twitched, and his balls tightened. Reluctantly, Alexa pulled back again. The tortured expression on his face was delicious, and she straddled his thigh, running her nails over his sac.

Alice pulled her fingers away as her pussy twitched. She had come so close. Alice made eye contact with John and grinned, a naughty idea popping into her head. She suckled on her fingers, watching his jaw clench. Alice leaned closer to John and kissed him, the taste of her moisture and desire clinging to her tongue. Alexa felt his whole body stiffen beneath her. John was reaching his breaking point. She lowered herself down on his cock a final time, and the veins in his neck distended as he struggled with his self-control.

"Alexa, fuck. No, I'm…" His words were strangled, and he thrust his hips, groaning, and no longer in control of himself. John didn't allow her to pull away this time, his hands holding her in place. He thrust into her hard and fast, watching her breasts bounce and her eyes close as she derived pleasure from his roughness, Alice's scent still in his nose, and her taste still on his lips. He felt his climax build. His cock was hot and heavy. Alexa's body clamped around him, milking him, tightening as she matched his rhythm. When she came again, Alexa threw her head back, a growl stuck in her throat, her nails digging into the skin of his thighs as she held him in place. Her pussy clamped around his cock. John gripped her hips tighter and increased his speed. He followed her soon after. His orgasm tore through him with so much force that he went dizzy from it. Alexa exhaled a shaky breath and lay on top of him; his cock still twitching inside her pussy. She kissed his neck and giggled happily. Alexa rolled off of him, panting, grinning, and running her fingernails lightly over his chest.

"Daddy?" Alice asked.

John looked at her through a haze and noticed the wild look in her eyes. Alice had followed Alexa's order and hadn't finished herself off.

"Can I cum now?" She asked. Alice was squirming uncomfortably, her pussy glistening with her moisture, coating her thighs and pooling beneath her.

"You've been such a perfect girl, Alie," he said. His cock was still hard and twitching, cum dribbling from the head. Alexa had pushed John over the edge, but the build-up had been so much that his cock was still hard. Alice was drunk with lust and edging.

"Come here, baby girl," John said, stroking his wet cock.

Alice crawled her way over to him, licking her lips as she watched his hand tug on his shaft. She stopped in front of him, still on her hands and knees.

"Stay just like that," he said, getting on his knees behind her.

Alice obeyed, glancing over her shoulder at him as he positioned himself behind her. Alice was shivering in anticipation. A surprised yelp escaped her lips when John tugged lightly on the tail of the butt plug that was still inside of her ass. Alice moaned as her body burned for him.

"Please, Daddy." John wrapped the fur of the tail around his forearm, gently tugging on it, eliciting soft whimpers of pleasure from his little girl. Alexa lay on the carpet, watching them, enjoying the sight. She was spent, her body tingling from her orgasms and her headlight. He thrust his cock into Alice's waiting pussy and groaned as a new wave of pleasure rocked him. Alice pushed back against him, letting his cock fill her, gently wiggling herself onto his cock as she adjusted to his size. She began rocking against him, causing the length of the tail to tighten and release rhythmically around his arm. Alice was filled to the brim, unable to control herself anymore. After a moment, letting Alice set the rhythm, John matched her speed. He made long, slow thrusts as Alice gyrated against him. She let herself go, her body relaxing, taking his cock as deep as it could go. Her ass was filled with the butt plug that John tugged on to remind her that it was still there. Not that she needed the reminder. With the length of the tail wrapped around his forearm, every thrust reminded her, and the smallest movement sent a shock of pleasure through her ass and pussy. The sensations built upon each other and set her heart beating rapidly as her desire grew with each thrust.

"Faster," Alice said, too delirious to form full sentences. Her breathing was fast, and her head swam with thoughts of her Daddy pounding his cock deep into her dripping pussy. John grinned at her quiet request. He increased his speed a little with each thrust, not wanting her to reach her orgasm too quickly. Alice was whimpering, clawing at the carpet, by the time Alexa had collected herself. She was watching the two of them from the sidelines, blissful and satisfied, their combined scent clinging to her skin.

"Tell Daddy what you want, Alie. Tell Daddy how much you want him," Alexa said, rolling onto her side, lazily stroking herself. John's cock swelled and throbbed inside Alice's pussy as he listened to her moan and pant. He kept his pace steady, drawing out her pleasure as she stretched her arms out in front of her, pressing her breasts into the floor, arching her back.

"Please." It was all Alice could get out. Her mind was flooded with lust and desire, only focusing on one thing.

"I want you to fuck me, Daddy," Alice said. John increased his pace, and Alice's answering grunt told him she was close. He thrust into her, her pussy stroking his cock and tightening around his shaft with each quick thrust. Alice's eyes closed as her pleasure stacked. She was so close that if he stopped right now, she would burst into tears.

"Fuck!" Alice screamed as she finally came. Her body twitched violently, her pussy tightening around his cock and her ass doing the same with the butt plug. Her scream turned into loud whimpers. Her eyes closed, and her breathing was ragged.

John kept his rhythm as Alice tightened around his cock. Her pleasure warmed him, causing a familiar feeling in his balls. He was gasping for breath, sweat beading on his brow.

Alice moaned again as her orgasm slowly tapered out, and John pulled his cock in and out of her twitching pussy, loving the feel of her body's pleasure. He pulled himself out, and Alice moaned in protest. John chuckled and thrust back in, taking her hard and fast, fucking her until he thought of nothing but finishing inside of her wet, tight pussy. John grunted, forcing himself to pull out seconds before he came. Hot streams of cum spurted over her ass and back, matting into the fur of the tail.

John swayed behind her, slowly stroking the last few drops of his cum from his cock.

Alice moaned in satisfaction, stretching herself out on her belly. John lay down next to her, trailing a hand over her back, drawing circles on her skin, raising goosebumps in his wake. Alexa scooted closer, sandwiching their little girl between them. She kissed her nose and pushed Alice's dark, wild hair from her face. Her cheeks were flushed, and her eyes glazed over, a soft smile on her lips, and there was a hint of a dimple in her cheek.

"I think we should get cleaned up, don't you?" Alexa said, and Alice giggled.

"But I'm sleepy," she said.

"I know, baby girl." Alexa murmured, lacing her fingers through Alice's.

Alice reluctantly sat up. She took Alexa's offered hand and rose to her feet slowly, her head feeling as though it was tenuously filled with helium and attached to her neck by a string. Her pussy was still twitching, and her legs weak as she gingerly took a step. Her head swirled dizzyingly, and Alexa caught her, laughing.

"S'not funny," Alice mumbled, but she smiled despite herself.

"Of course you are, baby girl. You're the funniest and the sweetest," Alexa said and kissed her cheek.

Alexa got into the tub with her and hugged her close as the warm water soaked into them. Their scent mingled with the fruity aroma of the bubble bath Alice had chosen. Alexa combed her fingers through the ends of Alice's hair.

"That's nice," Alice said sleepily.

"Did you have fun, Alie?" Alexa asked.

"Yes, Mommy. Did I do good?"

"You did well, baby. You were such a good girl." Alice grinned, "Really?"

"Really," Alexa confirmed, and she kissed the top of her dark hair. The buns had come undone, and the ribbons were hanging limply. Alexa gently untied the knots and set the ribbons on the edge of the tub.

"Can we have ice cream later?" Alice asked as Alexa brushed her fingers through her hair again.

"Of course, but only after dinner."

"Aw," Alice said, pulling a face and sticking her tongue out.

"You know the rules, baby," Alexa said, smiling softly.

"I know, Mommy."

"Can we watch cartoons while we eat?" Alice asked after a few moments.

"Yes, we can," Alexa said and snuggled her face into Alice's neck. Alice giggled and hugged Alexa's arms to her breast.

"I had fun today, Mommy," Alice said.

"I'm so happy to hear that, baby girl. I had fun, too."

"I'm glad that I met you and Daddy," Alice said, turning her head so she could nuzzle Alexa's neck. Alexa smiled, Alice's words making her heart thump in her chest.

Alice scooted forward in the bath and handed the bottle of bath gel to Alexa. "Can you help me wash my back, please?" Alexa grabbed the gel, and the giant strawberry-shaped sponge Alice had picked out. The gel made a generous lather, and Alexa gently scrubbed Alice's skin.

"Stand up," Alexa said. "But be careful. Use the support bar."

"Okay, Mommy." Alice stood, glad for the non-slip mat that Alexa had put in just for her. The bath oils Alice had bought on a whim were notorious for making the tub a slippery bowl of death. Alexa gently scrubbed between Alice's legs, running down the inner thigh and back up again in small circles. Alice shivered, cooling down from their play.

"I think we should make waffles for dessert," Alice said, already thinking of covering the whole thing in ice cream and caramel syrup.

***

"Daddy!" Alice squealed. She bounced towards him in the kitchen where he had dinner prepared and was setting the table, her koala tucked under her arm.

"Careful, baby girl. This stuff's hot."

"What did you make, Daddy?" Alice asked, toning down her excitement and plopping into a kitchen chair. She dropped her head in her palms and watched as he set out serving spoons and a huge bowl of salad.

"Cottage pie," Alice happily clapped her hands together. The jostling made Beanie fall from her arms. Alice's robe was slightly too big for her, the sleeves covering her hands. She flapped them and giggled again. She was sleepy and very, very comfortable. She carefully hopped off the chair and collected her koala, setting him in his chair.

"Daddy, can I make a place for Beanie?" Alice asked.

"Yes, you can, but wait for me to help you, okay?"

"Okay, Daddy," Alice said, still flapping her one, sleeved arm like a lopsided little bird.

***

Alice pulled John by the hand to the small table in the corner of her room. Alexa leaned in the doorway, watching over them, her heart light.

"Don't stay up too late, Alie," she said and gave John a meaningful look and pointed at her watchless wrist.

"Don't let her sweet-talk her way into an extra hour, or you'll be in trouble, too." Alexa winked and left them to their fun. Alexa had some work to tend to before Monday and didn't want to do it tomorrow while Alice was awake.

"Yes, Mommy." Alice fluffed up her pillow and dropped into it.
John followed suit less gracefully. "What do you want to do?"

"This!" Alice said and pulled a medium-sized box from the shelf beside her, setting it on the table. It was filled with multi-colored blobs of clay and playdough wrapped in cling wrap or stuffed into ziplock bags. Alice turned the box over, dumping the contents onto the table. After a few minutes of rummaging through the packages, she huffed, "I'm out of green."

"What do you want to use green for?" John asked.

"I wanted to make grass." Alice pouted.

"Well, there's a little trick I learned when I took a semester of art theory in college," John said and grabbed a big pinch of yellow and one blue. When he squashed the two colors together, Alice let out a yelp of surprise.

"No! No, Daddy! I'm not allowed to mix them!" Her voice was high and shrill, genuinely panicked.

"Don't worry, baby girl. I'm helping you so that Mommy won't get mad."

Alice frowned, "But..." John cocked his head at her and pulled a funny face, "If Daddy says it's okay, Mommy won't get mad, baby."

"Okay, Daddy," she said.

John showed her how to mix the two different colors well so that they didn't make swirly yellow and blue streaks in random spots, adding in a little bit of blue to make it a shade or so darker. When he was done, there was a light green tint to the palm of his hands, and Alice laughed.

"Here you go, Alie," John said proudly.

Alice took the lump from him and inspected it.

"Good job, Daddy," Alice said, nodding her head. She rolled the clump of green clay into a long thin snake, showing her Daddy how to make sure it was even all over, breaking off pieces when they were just the right thickness and length to pass as grass. Every so often, Alice stopped to inspect John's handiwork, nodding, and letting him continue. When she was satisfied that there were enough little green bits, she showed him how and where to place the little blobs of clay-grass on the wooden board she was using for her sculpture. They did end up staying up way past her bedtime, but John and Alice had managed to finish their happy little diorama.

"This is you," Alice said. "This one is Mommy."

"Where are you?" John asked, peeking around the back of the small, lopsided house.

"Over here, silly." Alice giggled and pointed out her clay stickman standing right in the middle of the two giant people that towered over the house.

"Oh, now I see! You did such a good job, baby girl."
Alice threw her arms around him and crawled into his lap, yawning.

"Thank you for playing with me," Alice said. John wrapped her in a tight hug, "Any time, baby girl." He gently rocked her, humming her favorite song, listening as her breathing changed and she fell asleep in his arms.

Who is Tina Moore?

Tina Moore has enjoyed the lifestyle of a Mommy Domme for several years. She began secretly exploring kink and BDSM in her youth and found her love of being a strict Mommy Domme in early 2000. Tina Moore slowly became more comfortable and confident through making friends in the community and exploring the lifestyle and now openly celebrates being a Mommy Domme to her little.

Before becoming an author, Tina Moore worked in the finance sector, but it was through the encouragement of her current little that she took the leap and wrote her first MDLG book, Nancy's Little One.

From then on, Tina Moore continued to combine her experiences and desires, as well as the sweet and naughty things her baby girl does, to bring you tantalizing and salacious stories about both MDLG and DDLG relationships and the ABDL littles and middles who enjoy them.

Follow her on:
Author Page on Amazon
Instagram @tinamoore.kdp

www.ingramcontent.com/pod-product-compliance
Lightning Source LLC
Chambersburg PA
CBHW030756190726
48285CB00003B/889